I0450936

LIONS AMONG HUMANS

Not For Kids Vol. 2

Part 2

JORGE HARRINGTON

Jorge Harrington

DEDICATION

Dedicated to my good friend Daniel Frank

INTRODUCTION

This is Volume 2 of the Not For Kids Series. One that I am glad to say is a lot better than my first book, because I took my time with this one and have dived a little deeper into the character's lives a little more.

Picking up where it left off from The Broken Pane. Obviously my first story to tell, but with each story to come, I and the story gets better and better. I want to thank you for taking the time to read this introduction, and of course for reading the book in your hands.

Reading is my passion, and to write a book like this, or any book, makes my love for the act that much greater. I hope that I will one day be a successful author that has lines of people lining up to get my signature. Yes I am a dreamer. It keeps me committed to reach my goal, because everyday that I write words on the computer makes me better in fulfilling my dreams. It is hard being a self published author, trying to get my work out in the world, and getting the honest reviews that will help me in the future. Though it is hard, I still want to continue doing this, till I have passed from old age.

I hope you enjoy.

Sincerely,

Jorge Harrington

Lions Among Humans

Support an author instantly by leaving a review on Amazon.com. Put the name Jorge Harrington in the search bar and click the title of your choosing, then leave an honest star review. This honestly is the best way to help local or popular authors, and I just want to say thank you for taking the time to read not only this book, but leaving a review for me. Keep on reading, thank you from the bottom of my heart.

You can contact me by email, Twitter, Facebook, or Instagram. All that information is

jorgeharrington032089@gmail.com

Jorge Joseph Harrington on Instagram

@geobonii on Twitter

ACKNOWLEDGMENTS

This is my second go around with writing. I would first off like thank my wife Kristen for giving me my three sons, I do this for you. My mom Johnnie, my sisters Olivia, Amelia, Tana, Halley and my brother Leighton.

In my first book, I have thanked a majority of my friend, and that It would fill up another book if I were to write all their names in the acknowledgments of the page. Well I will be naming some names that might have not made it into the book. So here they are. I want to thank: Chucky, Josheph, Roy, Randall, Jack, Amanda, Mari, Mary, Kathy, Kindall, Jeannine, Jackie, Amber, Debra, Rebecca, Haley, Carmen, Ashley, Linda, and Tori.

There are so many more and I would like

to thank them all for being in my life, because they are the reason why I am the man I am today. I of course would have to thank the two kings, the king of horror and the king of hearts, Stephen King and Nicholas Sparks. I have read the most of both of your books, and I can't wait to read more from you.

I would also like thank my editor and cover designer Caelin. You are a Godsend, you are the first person to help me get these books looking and sounding the way they do.

Lions Among Humans

Not For Kids Vol. 2

Part 2

Lions Among Humans

CHAPTER

1

It was hot in the town of Plymouth. Making everything miserable and sweaty, the electric bills were definitely going up from the swamp coolers and air conditioners; being on all the time. Rachael and the twins were sitting under one of the machines; each room had their own, which was nice.

They were playing a game. One that had all the letters of the alphabet, numbers one through zero, a 'YES' and a 'NO', and two symbols that were in the shape of the moon and the sun.

"It'll be fine Barbara, quit being so scared. There is such a thing as doing safe OUJIA." Rachael said. She was pouring salt – the big grains of salt – around the board. "We have to have three people, you'll be writing down what it says on the board, and we have salt and holy water. Trust me, I read all this online. What could go wrong?"

Barbara, knew that her sister was telling the truth, so did Ella who had an empty sheet of paper and a pen. Even though she didn't say anything, Rachael knew that she was scared of her own shadow, and even though this sort of activity wasn't considered normal, it still was all fun and games.

"Just let me do all the talking, and you just write everything that I'm saying. Got it?" asked Rachael.

Barbara nodded her head, and began to write.

"Ella, no matter what, just rest your hands on mine. That way we can stay strong and don't get confused about who is pushing the damn thing. Got it?"

Ella too; nodded her head.

Rachael knew how to bless the water – did it at least seven times, so she knew for sure – and put the water in a little spray bottle, so the pressure can sting any demon that might find its way inside her, or her sisters. The salt she had was the kind you had to buy off the internet; she begged and threw a fit so she could use her dad's credit card for it. She was responsible about it, but you didn't really need to spend eight dollars – plus shipping and handling – just so you could play some witch board.

As long as the spirit was from the sun and not the moon, they were in the clear. Rachael wasn't too sure on the time, but it passed the time, and she wanted to speak to her mother. There was a movie on this sort of subject, but she never went to go see it. There was a picture of Elizabeth Figgs in a picture frame, standing on a pile of books next to the three sisters.

"Remember, if you hear anything in the house that is a loud noise, or if something moves, or if you hear any sort of voice, do not say anything. Let me do all the talking. Spirits can lie, and if it is our mom then let me be the judge of that." Rachael knew that besides her sister Ruth, the twins knew that they were taken care of no matter what.

Rachael moved the white cursor around in a clockwise motion. "Are you from the sun or the moon?"

There was no movement. Only Barbara who was moving her pen across her paper.

"Are you from the sun or the moon? We come to talk to our mother Elizabeth Figgs, is she present?"

The planchette still moved slowly in the same position Rachael was moving it, a circular motion that was easy and not too forced. Rachael repeated her mother's name. Only this time there was sudden jerk and then it slowly moved to the 'NO' word on the right side of the board. The sisters were a little confused with this answer, because they didn't know if it meant that they didn't come from the sun, or that they had no contact with the their mother.

She repeated again, only this time she pulled on the planchette; a smidgen, so she could get the answers she was looking for. But then it quite the circular motion, and started to hover across the board to the letter 'N', then right to the letter 'O'.

That too spelled the word 'NO'.

They must have been talking to the most stubborn and stupid spirit that ever walked the spirit realm. Maybe that's why they were dead and not alive. These were the thoughts that crept into the brain of the older sister. She tried to keep her mind clear, and think about why they were playing with the game in the first place.

The planchette moved to the sun symbol.

"Are you sure that you come from the sun?" Asked Rachael, she wanted to talk to her mother. Maybe she could haunt their house, and make dad come home after work once in awhile.

5

Truth was, the girls' dad was haunted by their mother ever since she died.

The next word was 'YES'.

"Are you my mother Elizabeth Figgs?"

'NO'.

"Can you please go get her; so I can speak with her?"

'M' 'Y' 'B' 'E'. Barbara wrote the word – *Maybe.*

"What does that mean? You either have to give me a *yes* or a *no* answer, you're not playing the game right spirit."

' S' 'R' 'R' 'Y'. Barbara wrote the word – *Sorry.*

"Don't be sorry, just either go get my mother or say something interesting."

Rachael looked at the salt circle, if there was any grain of salt out of place, or any imperfection in the circle, the spirit would come at them. But this was all just a precaution, an older sister being an older sister. Even if the situation was considered silly.

A few seconds of the planchette moving around, was making Barbara a bit dizzy. Then it started spelling again.

'M' 'M' 'G' 'N' 'E' 'O'N' 'Y' 'M' 'E'. Barbara wrote a few words this time, which were – *Mom Gone Only Me.*

Rachael knew that after all the game shows she watched, like FAMILY FUED, HELLEVATOR, and CHAIN REACTION, to know that the spirit was telling her that her mother was gone and only it remained.

"That's a lie, because you can't be the only one there. I bet its crowded down there."

After all that talk about playing the game safe, was starting to go out the window. Rachael caught herself and said she was sorry. Then continued to speak to the spirit named 'ME' in a calm voice again. "Is Elizabeth available to talk to?"

'G' 'N' 'E'. Barbara wrote the word – *Gone.*

"Okay, I guess I will talk to you then, you

seem to be so chatty anyways."

There was a noise of water spouting out across the house. Ella looked to that direction, trying to keep calm and not to push on the planchette, but then remembered not to pay any attention to other noises when in contact with the dead.

"Is ME you real name?"

'NO' 'M' 'R' 'M' 'R'. The words were tricky, but she came up with – *No Mister, Mister, or No Murmur.*

Barbara wrote the letters down, but couldn't make them.

"Murmur?" Said Rachael out loud. But then caught herself when she did. You are never to say a demon's name out loud no matter what. It would summon itself to the one that spoke the name. That was when Rachael noticed that the salt was still intact.

Then the door swung open and caused a breeze to stir up, that made the salt go across the board and onto the carpet. All three girls looked up at their sister Ruth, who was in a pink towel and had a huge smile on her face.

"Hello girls, I just wanted to say that I got off work early. I have something I wanted to tell you, something that might change my life, as well as yours." Ruth said. She was leaning against the door frame looking, then saw that they were playing a really scary game.

"Where did you get that?"

"We got it under dad's bed, he has all kinds of stuff. Things that he will never use again, I thought this would be tons of fun. Then you went ahead and ruined it, a demon is in the house now." Rachael was happy to see Ruth, but gave her a mean look.

"I highly doubt that, but I know your gonna have to get the vacuum to clean up all that salt. Why did you pour salt all over the floor?"

"Salt is an act of God you know, it repels demons, but now its all over the place and we didn't tell it goodbye, so now the house is haunted."

Ruth looked at her sister with a raised

eyebrow. She never would have thought her sister was a nerd for this sort of shit.

"Well Rake is going to be here later today to have dinner. Please don't act like that when he's here."

"You mean dad's friend. Isn't that a bit creepy?"

"I guess from your point of view it could be, but that's the reason he coming over to tell you guys something. So put the game away, and get ready." Ruth had left the doorway before anyone could answer. It would have been Rachael, because still the twins didn't say much.

Ella and Barbara both looked at their sister with those eyes. Ones that were wondering about; if what she said about the house being haunted was true.

Rachael just gave them a nod, letting them know that she would never lie to them for as long as she lived.

* * * * *

CHAPTER

2

"Why did you do such a thing like that sir? She was a woman for Christ's sake!"

"Hen, you don't know what I just saw. It was something we have read out of some book. But that's all they are books. Little papers with nonsense written on them, crammed together, so we are able to flip through it." John was staring at his help, with little diamonds of sweat forming on his temples. A point was coming, Henry knew it. "Only I believe that woman was the reader that was here yesterday. I believe what I saw was something that isn't possible."

"Like what? You just struck that reader across the face and she left running out of the mansion." Henry usually was the brave one that stood up for himself, no matter if he was let go from his job. Only this time – seeing violence for the first time, in a long time – he decided to keep certain words in check.

"Hen, why don't you rewind the live feed, and see for yourself. You're the best at doing it anyways, go ahead. When you see it, then we'll talk." John sat down in his chair and wiped his face some tissue, otherwise he was going to have to get a new shirt, or take a shower.

Henry looked at his master with deep regret. He never in his whole life seen him like this, he always talked about his books in such a kind manner, like a boy falling in love for the first time. It was a huge shock indeed.

He left John alone, so he could go see the footage of the reader that too called herself October. There was something that bugged the poor old man, he scratched his head. He could have sworn she looked like the October that had some wrinkles around the eyes and mouth. But it was impossible. What was it that his master always said. If it wasn't there in the first place; it never existed. Something along the lines of that. Only this defined reality. Henry thought he was going to give himself an ulcer if he kept stressing over it.

When he reached the computer room, there was a small stack of discs that sat right about the main power source. It was a special shelf. It held all the footage for a twenty-four hour day on it. Once there was a month's worth of footage, it was filed away for future viewing. If someone were to find this, they might find five percent of interesting stuff, and ninety-five percent of two old men goofing off.

The footage Henry needed was only a few moments ago, so he pressed pause on the live, then grabbed a big black knob – sort of like a mini steering wheel – and turned it slowly to the right. The screens started to move in slow motion in reverse.

Finally he could see the niece of that one

reader, he pressed play, watching her move towards the back of the book hop. It was a long walk, considering how many books there were. Still after all these years it put him in awe, almost like the passengers when they saw the Titanic for the first time. It was all inspirational and overwhelming simultaneously.

All the cameras were set perfectly on her. The moment she stepped out of range, another one caught her in the lens. Normal stuff, this would've been right before he saw her coming down the hallway.

It wasn't normal though.

What Henry saw made him almost made his eyeballs pop out of his head. There seemed to be a creature riding on her shoulder. More like it was halfway out of her head.

"Do you believe me now?"

Henry was startled. If he hadn't checked clenched his toes inside his shoe – a nervous perk – he might have jumped right out of them. There in the doorway was John Silence. He rarely ever comes in this room, says the camera room is the only place he wouldn't feel safe, because there is no camera in the camera room.

"Sir, you almost gave me a sudden death."

"I apologize my friend, I love you. But I fear this is a time to be afraid."

Henry thought his master had finally gone the crazy he knew he would become one day. "Why would I need to be afraid sir?"

"You see that thing on that reader's neck? That there is a demon from the place of fire and fry, also known as Hell. I read in a book that when a deal is made with the Devil, invisible cracks form in the thin glass of reality. Things come through whether we like it or not."

"You're saying that thing is a demon?"

"It is a demon, there is no doubt about that. Cameras pick up everything my dear Hen, did you know? Did you really think I didn't have anything else to spend my money on? This is what killed my father all those years ago. Its hitched a ride with this reader, and now is in this house."

Henry's eyes switched back and forth, form the right eye to the left eye of his master. This man has been telling the truth to him, the moment he signed his first check. How dare he – now – ever doubt a man as wise as John Silence?

"The black thing must have gone back with the reader; when you sent her away?"

"No Hen, and that's not a niece of October. That is October, she is the one that made the deal. She has found a doorway to Hell – one of many! If you hadn't fought me off of her about that book, we might be the ones making a deal with good old Lucifer."

"The book!" Henry had a eureka moment.

"Very good Hen, but knowing myself and if I had it my way, I would be the one with his soul in Tim-buck-too. That reader is doing the work of the Devil."

"You don't know that sir. She could be some other girl for all we know, we don't even know where your niece is. How could you possibly come to that sort of accusation?" Asked Henry. All of a sudden the room they were in, felt like some sort of prison cell.

"Faith my dear Hen. I know because I have faith in what I've read, Horac is proof of that. Don't you remember?"

Yes, there was that. They had faith in a book they read from a few years back. The dog was living proof that they did indeed get rid of the cancer, then in another book, they built the wheels and the harness from scratch. It was a complete success, one that they were both confident to perform again if the situation asked for it.

"I believe you sir. That is why I have stayed beside you all these years, I have showed you my love and affection and plan to do so till the day I pass out of this world." Henry bowed to his master. If something like that were to ever happen in this time and age, he would be criticized for his actions.

But this act of kindness was from a book, and this John Silence knew it. It warmed his master's heart.

"Thank you Hen, I am glad to know that you will stick by my side, because I'm going to need you."

"Of course, sir. But for what?"

John closed the door and bolted the door shut. He knew that there were three things that man found important - no . . . scratch that . . . there were three things that some men thought were important in life. Those three things are money, time, and information.

Lucky for the master reader, he had all three.

"Why are you locking the door sir?"

"I told you that thing is in the house, and its inside Horac."

Henry's eyes were white for a moment, then they started to turn a shade of pink, as the old butler tried to fight the tears. That was his baby.

There was faint sound.

Both men listened, they could hear the beating of each other's heart. They could heart that and the sound of something being dragged. Louder and louder it came closer to the door, then stopped. It was the longest moment of stillness they have ever felt.

* * * * *

CHAPTER

3

The perfume was the right layer, not too thick and not too strong; once Rake got close enough to her neck, he would smell; what was called Red Lovely. Never had she felt like this, never had she felt like a normal girl, finally she didn't feel like a mother of three. Her makeup was light – she didn't need much – it made her feel desirable and seductive.

The two times they may love, played over in her mind. It was surprisingly how fast it happened. Ruth was drunk of the memory, it made her fell sensational, and all she did was bring him lunch. All the chips where on her side of the gambling table, and she needed to cash out before she lost. The only thing that a woman can do when nervous, is to look pretty doing it.

Jeans and shirt was all she could really come up with. Only she knew that Rake being the farmer that he is, would be in jeans and a button up shirt all the same. It helped with her worry, but she knew that being next to a man like Rake Blu, would probably make her slur her words or something to that extent.

What would her sisters think? They have met some of her boyfriends before. Ruth thought then she was in love with them, Rake was different. But they were boys, ones that only wanted to get into her pants. Rake was a man, and all she wanted was to get into his pants, Sex was the way of life. Amazing dopa-mine

It was Ruth who broke it off with them. Sometimes there was the occasional asshole that didn't take 'no' for an answer, but she knew a kick to the groin and a knife to his throat. Made all the difference.

But now she was older and more mature, not wanting boys anymore, not even the ones that were probably more attractive than her dear Rake.

She needed a married man. Rake was that man, he has been trough the ups and downs of love. All *she* had to do was the things *his* wife wouldn't do, like cook and have sex. The farmer had promised her, he would end it with his wife, who is named after a month. Then they can get to being happy.

"Now you're leaving us like mother and our stupid drunk of a father." Said a voice that was behind Ruth. It was the voice of her sister.

"I'm only going out for a little bit. Plus, I don't know when he'll be here, or where we're going, so you have me till then. We're are coming back here anyways."

"So you're a thing now? That was fast. He's old, and you act like you're in love with him."

Ruth didn't say anything right away. She checked to see if her boobs looked good inside her shirt.

"Well that means you love him."

"Will you please get out of my room? Its not like I'm leaving without cooking for you guys." Ruth was acting more like a sister then a mother now.

"Well that good . . . just kidding. When you go and don't come back. I guess I will tell the twins that you'd rather go get *some*, then take care of us."

"I never wanted to!" As soon as it left her mouth, Ruth was kicking herself in the ass all over again.

Rachael left the room not before giving a look, one that told her older sister 'I guess I'll be mother from now on, bitch', then she left the room.

Was Ruth being selfish? Or was she making something out nothing again? Stuck between a rock and a hard place, she continued to fix herself up regardless of what just happened. Little did she know it was going to be for nothing.

Below the camera room, there was a hidden floor to the house, it made it easier to get to the bookshelves that seemed to make up the floor that people walked on, they fit underground like trays of honeycombs. John and Henry were on another level of strange, when it came to books.

It was really dim down there, despite the lights emulating off the shelves and the floors.

"Get the live feed from camera 86, I wanna see if hat entity has done anything to Horac." John made sure that the trapdoor was heavily secure, before meeting Henry at his side. The thing was getting in no matter what, but the extra precaution might buy them sometime.

"What do you think you'll find sir?" Henry asked, he was now sitting at a desk that had the same set up; as the camera room upstairs. This was the back up.

Henry's question was answered, because when camera 86 was pulled up on the screen, there was the entity wearing the body of Horac.

Black claws have pushed its way out of the paws of the dog, needle like spikes pushed themselves out of the spine. One hug from it, would be nailed to it forever.

"My God! He looks like a snake, like the one who spoke to Eve in the garden." John said, peering into the screen.

"Snakes don't have arms."

"They used to, my dear Hen, have you not read the Bible?"

"I know about God, isn't that enough?" Henry was giving an unsure look at his master.

John gave a tsk-tsk, then began preach. "When Adam and Eve ate from the tree, God punished all that were countable. Eve's labor pains during child birth would be so severe that they could perhaps die birthing a baby. It was the serpent that told the first lie to Eve, and was forever moving along the Earth on it's belly. Then to Adam, God gave sin that leads to death and would pass to all mankind's children." That thing is so the devil can keep the fear in us."

The collar around Henry's neck was a pool of sweat. His face was flush and he looked grief stricken. Perhaps maybe in all the books Henry has read, there might be a chance to get out of this. Death was a necessity for all man, so why be afraid. Please not this way, any other way would be fine, but not this way.

"Yes my dear Hen, there is a way, I can see it in your eyes. We need to hurry. That thing has gotten through the door." Said John, looking at the screen that had a blizzard of pepper and salt also known as white noise.

"There is another story from the Bible, one that might help us exercise this demon from the house. Do you know how we do that Hen?" Henry shook his head slowly, then was startled by a knock on the trapdoor, almost making water run down his leg.

"We need an act of God, Hen. Lucky for us, we do have an act of God my friend. The Bible will keep us safe."

Henry clasped his hands over his eyes, wanting his master to get to the point already, before it got in.

"It started with Sodom and Gomorra, which was pelted with fire and brimstone. All died but a small family, they were given a safe passage out of the city, the family ran while the city burned. Lot and his wife and his two daughters, were given that opportunity as long as they didn't look back. They were to head for the hills and start their lives anew.

Only Lot's wife was the one that looked back, and was struck by God, turning her into a pillar of salt. That was an act of God

Henry peered over his master's shoulder and saw that the trapdoor was opened. A head came out of the hole in the floor with a toothy grin. Eyes that stared holes through walls, and claws that looked queer with Horac's skin over them.

Henry let out a scream and pointed, as he watched. The thing clambered towards them with such speed, that the stump; where the legs should have been, was making such a noise. It knocked over books off the shelves, kicked up dust off the floor, and cracked glass in the floors above. Right before it sunk its claws into the back John, he pulled out a salt shaker from his pocket. Quickly screwing the top off, and like throwing die; John threw it out at the airborne creature.

It gave a screech, as it exploded into a puff of red smoke, knocking the two men off their feet and into the desk with all the camera screens. Wires, glass, and the carcass of Horac was all over the floor.

A smell of burnt rubber and eggs filled the air, while the owner and the butler lay in a heap of each other. The body of Horac was like a bag with the bottom busted out and all the groceries spilled in each direction and up the walls.

"Sir?" Henry stirred. He felt pressure on his back, then realized that it was John. "Please! Are you alright?"

John rolled off the butler and lay like a sack of rice on the floor, there was blood in his mouth, coating his teeth like a film of red on white. Internal bleeding could cause that, perhaps even a punctured lung from the explosion. Henry would know, he was and still is a surgeon, it was his expertise. Blood poured out of the corner of his mouth all over Henry's arm.

The old butler instantly scooped up John like a baby, and began to wipe the liquid of perspiration and blood from the face of his master. There was a lot of the red liquid all over John's face, him bleeding out was driving the last nail in his coffin, and there was nothing Henry could do about it. Knowing his master's stubbornness, he was shut out of luck trying to get him to a doctor.

The owner's eyes looked up at the ceiling, then to Henry. "Do the research, you need to know what were up against, you need to help that reader."

"I need to help you-"

"Damn you Hen, you listen to me, I'm still alive and I still make the decisions. You hear me? You find the information and help that reader, I read all of this in a book once, and this can all go away."

Henry looked at John with eyes that didn't want to disappoint, but didn't know how to carry out his master's wishes John started to look like a child that had bonked his head on something, and was trying to Blood pooled around the two men; obvious now that it was coming from a cut in Mr. Silence's back.

"I'll try." Was all that Henry could squeeze out.

"That's a good Hen."

Henry wept bitterly, as he held the last of his family in his arms. John was dead.

＊ ＊ ＊ ＊ ＊

CHAPTER

4

When Rake pulled his truck into the driveway, there was a moment where he thought he was at a different house. Because this house looked like it came right out of a coloring book. The paint on the house was completely done away, it was gray old wood underneath. The roof was a sunken in the middle, with a huge crack up the front of it. Red light shown through a large gap then disappeared in a few seconds.

However, most of his attention was on the

whereabouts of Bruno and Einstein – force of habit – and all the anger and resentment he felt towards his wife came flooding back. Rake just knew that they weren't taken care of, or played with, or let off the chain. He even forgot to go get more dog food.

"Fuck." Was all that Rake could utter.

But when he started towards the horse trailer, the smell something dead and rotten, made him gag and cough. The pets must have caught a raccoon or a tiny animal, and hoarded the poor critter.

"Daddy's home. Who wants me to rub their belly?" Rake did a peek-a-boo motion into the trailer, but was knocked back like he had been hit with an uppercut.

Both dogs lay next to each other with lifeless eyes, ones that had life in them yesterday. Two of his loved ones were ripped away from him. *What happened? Did she go to such lengths as to murder his two babies in order to get back at him for being such an asshole?* Unlikely, but it was something to consider. If he knew that it would come to this, he would never had married the witch.

"October! You get your ass out her now!"

October had stopped her laughing, and just rubbed her baby bump. The feeling of having a child inside of her for the first time, made October do a silly dance, even though her stomach was heavy and well into the third trimester.

She felt full.

All the clothes she was wearing were torn up and reduced to rags and nakedness. October's belly button was hard and sticking out at the end. It hurt to touch it.

It was the book that brought her out of her celebration, fluttering open and closed, sounding like wings. October took the book from the table, holding the ends and bringing it close enough to see. Now that she was younger, no longer did she have to put the texts way out in front of her. It was a familiar feeling and magical feeling, to be reading up close.

Only for a few seconds did the pages remain blank, then names seemed to bleed out on the pages from within. There was a Rosemary Pike, and a George Clifford. These names meant nothing to October, perhaps the names of children that were robbed of their life, just like Sophia.

Flipping though the book with her thumb, the pages seemed to go on and on, for as small of book that it was. Suddenly, it got a mind of it's own, stiffening in the air, causing October to let go of the bound book. It didn't fall to the floor, instead it just stayed there like a ghostly podium.

Was this some "next step", to get this girl's soul to the devil?

A flash of red light tore out of the opened book, blinding October momentarily. *It had to be the next step*, because the light transformed into hands, almost an instant metamorphosis. They were bony, clawed, and misty hands. One hand grabbed her lower waist, keeping her still, while the other one came at her with such carefulness and a finger nail that could have been a knife. The finger made an incision down the front of October's stomach, similar to a blade cutting through a fresh apple.

It hurt like fuck. It mad October squirm frantically, but the hold on her waist keeping her from dropping to her knees. The little red apples moved out of the way as the hands reached inside October, helping them along with it's task. They crawled their way to the ends of the incision and pulled back on it, making it look like an autopsy on a cadaver. While some fell on the floor, rubbing their head in pain, others ran up and sat on October's shoulders and watched.

Who's red hands were these? Were they the actual hands of Lucifer?

It felt around like someone was fishing for a lighter in a purse. Then it hit home, it found what it wanted, and slowly it pulled. October felt like she had glass in her stomach, and the pulling felt like more glass was being shoved in. The little red apples were jumping out of the way, as the crater in October's belly got bigger.

Finally she could see a head . . . or a skull.

There was no flesh on the little girl anymore, October watched the bottom part of Sophia's mouth fall open as the head was all the way out. Then there was a rib-cage, then arms, and then soon there was legs. It was the first time October had seen a skeleton, and she felt okay with it.

There was another flash of red as the rest of the bones went into the book with a ripple. The hand that held her let go and followed the bones. October's belly was back to it's original state. Some red apples that didn't make it back in time, ran up and went inside the her nose and ears.

The list of names formed on the pages of the book, and a new name was added to it: SOPHIA SILENCE. Then the book slammed shut and fell to the floor.

Thud!

Silence? October recognized the name instantly. That could mean anyone though, some girl named Williams or Smith, the most common names in the United States, perhaps *ssilence* was the same. *So how could someone like*

Sophia Silence, be related to the man that had smacked her across the face not more than hour ago?

It was a very good question.

Regardless if she was related or not, October had eaten the girl and the feeling of satisfaction washed over. The soul was delivered to the other side, and getting revenge on John Silence would be the cherry on top of a perfect cake. She liked to think she hurt one of John's pupils on purpose.

Cute and isolated, October Blu no longer existed in this world, it was just a name with no meaning now, like the wolf in *Little Red Riding Hood* story. How the wolf became the Grandmother to lure the girl in the red hood right into the monster's belly, behind the horn rimmed glasses.

October was a named to be feared.

"October! Get your ass out here now!"

She knew that voice. It belonged to the man that had his cock buried in some ass, last time she saw him. He was also the man

October once called her husband.

While she peered out through the crack in the house – not noticing the house was in shambles, clutter, and smelled, even the hole in the house like another window to her. October could feel her body doing the same thing it did when she was lying on the porch. Another ten years just evaporated into thin air, this time her height was effected, she grew a foot more, because you shrink when you get older.

Never will she get older again.

Rake said it again, "October get your ass out here now!"

Never in a million years would he think that October could be capable of doing something like this. Both dogs looked like meat sacks, filled with broken bones and smashed insides. The more he looked at them, the more he believed she could do something this drastic.

In this world, there were people who

think pets to be children of the family. Then there are people who think pets are what they are. . . just animals. *What would he say to her? What would he do to her? If did anything, what would he tell people?* The answer would only reveal itself once he did any of them.

"I've been waiting for you?" Said a female's voice.

The old farmer spun around to find October, standing there on the porch. However, this woman looked to be a student finishing college, or was some damsel trying to get into trouble. She looked desirable and seemed to want to be saved by a knight in shining armor.

She wore a pink a robe, the exact one his wife owned, but it was the house that kept distracting him. It looked haunted, like a lost toy that had been tossed in the mud.

"Where have you been my love? I've been so worried." It said. There was no other way to explain her. It had the voice of his wife.

"Who are you? Where is October?" Asked Rake, he felt like he should cry.

"Its me October, don't you remember your own wife when you see her?" It replied.

"You're not my wife, October is way older than you, so old that she neglects her own pets. Bruno and Einstein." Said Rake, sarcastically.

"It was an accident my love, completely out of my control. It was you who led me to this new life, and with that I have no choice but to thank you."

Rake rubbed his eyes to see if he had gone nuts, he thought about giving himself a good smack across the face too. What the fuck was she talking about?

"Come into the house, I wanna give you something that I should have given you a long time ago." Then it went back into the house.

Rake watched as it moved without noise into the dark house.

Thinking about it, the girl did sort of resemble October, it was the way she stood there talking to him. Getting old was a bitch, because even though it was not more than ten feet from him, Rake still couldn't make out if it was his wife or not.

He did end up going inside the house after her. Thinking that if he could corner his wife into confessing that she killed Bruno and Einstein, the police would have her out of here in handcuffs.

Then there was a smell.

Moldy dairy products and something that smelled like peanuts, wafted in the air so thick, that Rake flinched by covering his nose with his whole arm. He went to the kitchen and threw open the door to the fridge, which was a stupid thing to do, because an invisible bomb of shit blew up.

"Don't mind that love, I can clean that up after I give you your surprise." It said, the voice was coming from the far bedroom.

Rake felt sick to his stomach, like the one you get when you see your first love after a huge break up. Ones that were ever truly in love would understand the feeling. That feeling is fear, a strong one that is difficult to shake. Time can heals all wounds, but that is if you decide not to kill yourself first.

It's voice was like a Siren.

Even though he didn't want to, Rake found himself in the hallway, going towards the bedroom. Why should he be scared? It was his house, his room, and his wife.

Not knowing the answer to his own question, Rake walked into his room, while he heard the last of the Lion's song: *If I Only Had The Nerve*, playing on the television.

★ ★ ★ ★ ★

CHAPTER

5

Henry had gotten some sheets from a cupboard upstairs, then laid it over John and Horac, which now were very peaceful in death. There would be no calling of the police, or some specialist to come and move the bodies to some freezer at a station. John wouldn't want that, he was too afraid of the outside world, too afraid for his own good.

He would have to find a place to bury him under the house, of course that would seem unnecessary, but Henry wanted to fulfill the needs of his dearest friend. Maybe have some wood delivered to the house and build a pine box for him and Horac, perhaps create a crypt. With a crypt, Henry would be able to bury himself with them.

Henry wiped the tears from his eyes. It was time to do what he was told to do, which was save the reader, but how? Only it was so obvious, there whole house was filled with book information, and the internet. The mess of the camera and computer equipment could wait for now, it was swept into a pile that he would later clean up, do the repairs to the house where it was needed, then find a place to bury Mr. Silence and Horac. Research needed to be done, and John's favorite book was *The Wizard Of Oz* – a good place to start – and there was no mystery of where that book would be.

The rosebush.

Not only was the camera that watched the master's chair it's whole life, the master's precious possession. John's childhood book, always better than the movie, was there. It withstood the winds of time and was a true classic.

It was either the Titanic or the Iceberg, when it came to books and movies, and you should always pick the iceberg.

There the book stayed inside a fireproof baggie, and it was holding the camera in place, here would be a start, John would hide his most valuable documents, in secret, but Henry knew what his master was up to. Knowledge was power, so was money, combined together you were hammering a nail with a hammer; instead of with a rock. The theory was good, but the execution of saving the reader was easier said than done.

Henry looked the eight by five book up and down, and *remarkable*; was all that he could think. This man kept this book in such great condition, that it looked brand new, there weren't any creases in the spine, or any thumb marks on the pages. Did John read this with tweezers?

When he opened the book, a folded piece of paper fell out on the floor. It wasn't a complete surprise to know that this was the

Will of John Silence. The real surprise was that he died in the first place, and that he was still fresh. Henry opened up the envelope and pulled out the precious document.

It read:

In case of my death, if accidental or by design, the property: including the land, house, businesses and The Broken Pane. Also the full amount of currency, either it be saved, taxed, or written off, will be inherited immediately – with the exception and under the guidance of Henry Fredrick – to Sophia Silence.

In case of the death of Sophia Silence, have it be accidental or design, or by the result of not responding to this Will in twenty-four hours upon reading legal documents. All the about mentions will be inherited immediately to Henry Fredrick.

A few words to who it may concern.

"I am what I am, because the death of my father. He was killed by a demon in the night, for a reason, only the monster would know. This fortune I own, comes with a package. All the stories in the Broken Pane are from all corners of the world, obtained by my ancestors. Some of which have

practiced the art of demonic communication, a scholar of the supernatural and scientists of the other world.

Reading only the experience of my grandfathers from past documents, I still have yet to see a demon or come across any likeness of the fallen angels. But the use of white noise can help see what cannot be seen with the naked eye."

Henry knew his master was paranoid, and a little security never hurt nobody, but this was an obsession with cameras. He read on.

"I could be a nervous old man, always watching my back, and trying to make sure there aren't any knives back there, so far there are none. Its funny, because I helped myself into my own grave; stress.

However, be warned there are books that have tales of such occurrences, and it would be foolish not to heed such warnings. Do the research and protect yourself with knowledge.

Knowledge is power."

Basically, John Silence was a nutcase that loved to read, and if Sophia wasn't found within twenty-four hours, Henry would be a damn rich man.

Its was sad though, knowing that he was going to get the fortune no matter what. Where was his master's niece? How was he going to save October Blu?

John's voice came into Henry's head, telling him that he needed to do the research and be ready. What book would he go looking for?

Henry heard the doorbell ring. Not the bell in the Broken Pane, the one that was at the main entrance to the house. Then like being struck by lightning, or zapped with static electricity. Henry believed that this might be a lead he could go on, and be able to carry out John's last wish after all.

Sometimes opportunity knocks, and sometimes opportunity rings.

Ella just watched as her two older sisters argued back and forth, while Barbara wondered how someone can scream and fight, while cooking over a hot stove and not burn themselves. Hopefully not spill the dinner all over the floor.

The twins sat at the table and watched Rachael and Ruth go at it. Seeing a scene like this helped boost their confidence, because they haven't said a word to anyone ever since their mother had died, and their older sisters gave a ray of hope, that one day they could have a screaming match just like this one.

Despite being silent, they knew that Ruth has every right to go and date with whoever she wanted, and need to stand with Ruth against Rachael. Except both Barbara and Ella kept finding ways to keep silent.

Food was placed in front of both of them, cheesy potatoes over fried steak, with green beans on the side. Here was a chance to say "thank you" but the twins held their tongues, and listened to the fight go on about that man that was here the night before.

"I'm not leaving you guys!" Screamed Ruth. "He's coming here."

"Oh, so now he's coming here to live?"

Asked Rachael, knowing quite well what her sister meant.

"Why can't you just let me have one night with him?"

"He's an old man for Christ's sake, what are your babies going to look like?"

"Why are you so mean?" Ruth had her fork pointed at her attacker.

"I learn it from you, because you're going to bring him into your life, so you can push us out."

Luckily, the fork went into the potatoes. Ella could tell that Ruth was done, because silence was also a weapon. It gave off the right vibe and unspeakable language that meant 'I'm so pissed and I could wish death upon you'.

Soon there was more fighting, for now, they ate like a peaceful family again. Sisters together is like an army.

No one heard the creaking sounds that came from the OUIJA board, it traveled through the walls, up into the ceiling, and was flying around the house like a vulture.

When Rake stepped into the room, he found the girl with the pink robe on that was almost the size of a tent on her. She also had the voice of October, and she acted like she lived in this house many of years. Her face was towards the window.

"What took you so long?" It asked.

"If you haven't noticed," Rake replied. "The house looks like a bomb went off in it. Did you see the fridge? It looks like shit city in there and it stinks so bad. The house has a hole in the wall. What have you been doing? Bruno and Einstein are dead!"

Rake was waiting an explanation, one that would make his head do the Exorcist head spin, but it didn't happen. Before anything could happen, the girl dropped her robe to the floor. Exposing a beautiful body he hadn't seen in what seemed a lifetime ago. It was October's alright, he knew by the birthmark on the right breast, but he must be drunk to think that his wife was in her twenties again.

It took everything for the old farmer to not drop to his knees.

With her breasts out and her hands on her hips, October looked Stunning. Like an old black and white cartoon, Rake rubbed his eyes with his closed fists, to see if the sexy naked girl would disappear. She didn't. October almost forty years younger and stood in her birthday suit, like she did when he first made love to her.

"What do you think my love?" It asked.

"I . . . you . . . how?"

"What does it matter? That tiny voice that says that this could be real. You may want to listen to it because it speaks the truth."

"I don't know what to say to you October." Said Rake, hesitantly.

"Don't say anything at all. Just lie down, because I want you inside of me."

Did she just say that? Wondered Rake, this girl who acted like his wife, resembled his wife, and sounded like his wife, wanted him to fill her up. He of course had already had sex with the Figgs girl, twice. The dirt and mud on his jeans, had already dried and fallen off leaving a gray and brown stain behind on his skin and pants.

Could he have sex for the third time? Only a fool would ask a question like that, plus he was supposed to be telling her that the marriage was over, and he had found someone new. Rake guessed that it could wait until after they had go "it" on. It was an unwritten rule, to not to tell, until after she had spread her legs. Of course he could have sex for the third time. He may be old and tire out easily, close to killing over – *almost* – but he could perform.

"What are you waiting for? Take off them clothes, plow *this* field for a change." It said.

How could she be talking like this? Rake was doing just as she asked, unbuttoning his shirt, then his pants, and then he was ready.

God worked in mysterious ways, and this was a result of that labor. All the emotions that he was feeling were on pause, yes; even the sad death of his two dogs, Bruno and Einstein, they were instantly put on the back burner. Rake just gazed upon the maiden on the bed.

He knelt down on the bed, and felt up the legs of October. *Gosh, what a beautiful name she was given.* He leaned close and kissed her lips, caressing her cheek. He couldn't leave this woman, never. Why would he think of such a thing?

Ruth's voice came into his head for a moment, while he kissed October over and over. It reminded him of that time he told Ruth that he loved her, and they were going to be together. Like a breeze, the voice came and went, and no one knew what time it was either.

"I want you inside of me so bad." It persisted. Clawing at his back. It may have felt good if he was in his twenties again like this impostor, but it felt like hell.

Rake did what he was told, and entered her.

The sensation he felt was amazing. Finally,

he was doing what he wanted to do with
October all along, and it felt like
Christmas – which was all he could come up
with to explain these feelings.

It was short lived though, because there
was a pain that shot up his groin and up into
his back. It paralyzed him in place, and his
breathing was short and fast, like he was
gasping through a straw.

He couldn't turn his head to look away
from it, but his eyes looked down at the thing
that had a hold on him. Yes, it was a thing
now, that had a dead look in it's eyes, and the
hair on it's head was growing and wrapping
around Rake's body, and attaching themselves
to the walls of the room.

Some ripping sound, came from the flesh
of October's belly, and then there was a tear;
right before Rake's eyes. Little red apples
spilled out all over the bed, then marched
about on the sheets. October's head just laid
there like she was unconscious and an empty
stare. The gaze was none the less pointed in
his direction, where he felt shivers go up his
back. Or was that those red things that came

out of their cocoon?

Like a rapid vine, the pain grew inside his body, ripping and tearing his insides.

Rake needed to move or do anything at this point. When he finally was looking down, after such strong will and exhaustion, he could see that his penis – still inside October – was no longer there. His member was absorbed and his back legs were coming up off the bed and going towards the direction of the ceiling.

Those red things that came out or her, were now licking the tears off Rake's face, some fell down inside his mouth, like it was all accidental on their behalf. As if they didn't read a sign that read:

CAUTION

MAY FALL IN DUE TO SLIPPERY
SURFACE

October's body was like a mouth now, the rib cage was the teeth, and all the external organs maneuvered themselves around to form a face inside. The nipples on her perfect beasts blinked and such, as if it hadn't tasted something like this before.

Slowly Rake was being shoved into a hole that wasn't big enough for his huge frame; his body was made of. He got stuck for a moment, but soon was all the way home. The screams were drowned out from October's blood still cramming their way down his throat, like a fun water slide. They went down to the bottom. Other red apples were jumping up and down on the back of the old farmer, so they can hoard their new piece of property.

Then it was all over. Right before the thought came into Rake's mind, to ask if this horror was ever going to end, it did. Now October lay on the bed, and looked like she did when she had eaten Sophia, but now she was twice the size now. Just like before, October was transforming in reverse, going back to the form she was when Rake had seen her. She did say she wanted him inside of her, and she was more than filled up. October was stuffed.

The hunger was still there though, only it was sleeping now, and October was drifting off to sleep, like anyone who eats a big dinner.

Having done the nasty with the one she loved, then devouring him, can make anyone dead tired. She was a black widow. One that was cunning, attractive, and sly. Two flies caught in her web, and all she had to do was put her faith in the lumberjack.

Her eyes closed and she slept awhile.

* * * * *

CHAPTER

It was getting to be that time again, Richard thought. The last of the customers were gone, the books were all accounted for, and everyone seemed to be checking out them books and returning them like they would any other day. Now, it was the hard part, choosing if he was going home to his girls, or go to Swers Bar like he did religiously.

He was hungry, Richard was kind of feeling like a Signature from Swers, only that would mean he would have a beer. There was nothing wrong with having a beer, no sir. Richard could even buy a six pack and bring his beer home, so he could actually spend sometime with his offspring, be involved. Making the choice that could possibly jog his memory into being a father.

"I don't know, I'll know when I get in the car and start driving." Richard said to himself.

The CLOSED sign was hanging in the doorway, lights off, and now he was behind the wheel. He was going to call home to see if the girls were okay, but that signal that they put into cars now, made sure that he couldn't receive or make any calls from his cell. All thanks to his dead wife.

Thinking that way was going to get him into trouble with his girls. Because he parked his car in the same spot he always did, the spot that was in front of Swers Bar. Richard got out and looked at his phone, and saw that he only had five percent left of battery, not enough to call home and have one of the girls talk him out of drinking.

"I'll make it up to them." Richard said out loud, as if it were a prayer to a God. Because he seemed to be the only one that cared about his situation.

Big Shop seemed to be so quiet around this area of the building, which was so crazy to think about. Actually, it really wasn't. The ones that had a drinking problem were the only ones that showed up here, and he wasn't about to put a damper in his attendance record.

When Henry had opened that door, he thought he might find a lawyer, or an old family member of John's. He would tell them that Mr. Silence had passed away, then they would ask if there was anything that he left out of his Will, they would tell him because he – as of right now – had control of the fortune.

The power of money can be very persuasive.

A series of locks and bolts were unlocked, and there was a small pause from the butler. If he ever opened this door to anyone without looking at the cameras first, John would've scolded him. No more scolding though, so sad days.

Was that a good thing, or a bad thing?

There in the frame of the front door, stood a man that was a bit overweight, but might have worked out at one point. Spikes were in his hair, made up with too much gel. Then a reddish beard that grew too much to one side, but the Hispanic male didn't seem to care about his appearance.

A uniform that was purple and black, on the chest pocket, there was two white initials: J. H.

"May I help you sir?"

"Yes you can, but first could I say that you have an amazing house here." Said JH, as he looked at the roof and took in a bit of fresh air as he looked. There was a box in his arms, "I work a website called: I DONT PLAY GAMES, one that you have recently subscribed to."

All Henry could do is just stare at this man with such wonder, surely he had to be pulling his leg. Who works at a place named something like that."

"Well you didn't buy anything, but you have a box here that you receive for signing up as a new customer. Its a box of the latest books that have been donated from the customers that have changed their mind at the last minute. Because once something is bought, even if it hasn't been handled, the value automatically goes down.

If you would have read the contract that you agreed to follow, which I'm pretty sure you didn't, no one ever does." The laughter coming from JH was sarcastic, but funny nonetheless. "Its fine, if you would be so kindly to take this off my hands, and sign on my little clipboard, I will be on my way."

The box was thrust into Henry's chest a bit hard, only it wasn't meant to be rude, right on top of it was the clipboard and a pen. The butler signed the paper, the one with the company's logo on it, and right below the name was a phrase from the founding fathers, it read like, "*Do you think this is a game?*"

"What books are in the box?" Asked Henry?

"Its all on the list, you'll see when you open it. It is a pleasure doing business with you, I guess I'll see you when I see you, oh and next time you need to read the agreement." Said JH, then he strode off the steps of the massive house, and got into his vehicle and sped away.

Henry had watched as he waved out the window to him as he drove on, but soon found himself in the house with a blade in hand, then cutting the tape off the box. Brown paper filled up the empty spaces, then sure enough, a list of all the contents inside.

Except it wasn't a list, it was piece of paper with only one title written on it. : *Dr. Sleep*.

It had been only fifteen minutes, and Richard had bought a Signature and two drafts, and was finished with one of them. The food always tasted so much better with beer, and the low mediocre music that played in the background, made it all the better. Some girls would be alright too. He decided to buy the first lady that walked in a drink, in hopes of getting lucky.

Someone did walk in, except it was no girl, but a young man with shoulders that were very broad for is jacket. A suit jacket that is, with a blue tie that complimented the black attire. He went up to the bar and ordered two drinks, a Long Island Ice Tea and a draft to chase it all down. The man could have sat anywhere in the bar, only he sat in front of Mr. Figgs.

"Can I help you?" Asked Richard, he had his glass dangling between his thumb and his pointer finger.

"I guess if you want to, I'm just sitting here because you look like you got a lot on your mind." said the stranger.

Richard gave out a laugh, and drank the rest of his glass. "I have a lot of things on my mind, but there is no way in hell you can understand what I've been through."

"My name is Daiye by the way, and I you're right, I will never understand." Daiye took a long gulp off his tea before he continued to speak. "There is a way I can understand how you feel. Only you'll feel like a ton of bricks fell on top of you, and I'm not sure you want that from me."

"What are you talking about? You can't just come up and start talking to a complete stranger, and start making statements like that." Richard gave a motion to the bartender. Which meant two more beverages would be on their way to the table.

"Why not? The old lady talked to the prince in the movie: *Beauty and the Beast.* When he didn't listen, he was transformed into what he really was, a beast." said Daiye. His drink was slowly receding.

"I must be drunk already, because you just compared us to a cartoon. Too bad you're not a girl, I got my beer goggles on."

"All I want to do is have a friendly conversation with you. I'm not a stranger anymore because I told you my name, and you see that we are drinking and exchanging words together. You haven't even told me your name."

"Richard. What did you mean that there is a way, and it'll hit me like a ton of bricks? You're weird bro."

"You have no idea." Said Daiye, he smiled and gave a wink of the eye.

"Okay, tell me then, hit me like a ton of bricks."

There was a slight hesitation from Daiye, then he of course was the one that brought it up. Not intentionally but he thought this man – *Richard* – would also be interested in the philosophy of philosophy, conversation is good for the soul. He was of course wrong, but it hadn't been the first time he used his abilities on someone that was so damaged.

"Are you ready?"

"I'm as ready as anyone. You must have a

story to tell."

"I do, but I won't tell you it, only, I can show you it. You'll show me who you are in the process, and there might be a mixture of emotions, and I will have to decipher which is mine and which is yours. Alright?"

Before anything could begin, Richard's drinks were brought to him. The bartender seemed to go into the back and didn't return for a little while. The whole bar seemed to be empty now, except for the stranger and the drunken father. Music in the background was *Journey*, and that was what they were about to go on.

Daiye reached out and grabbed the hand of Richard, and there was a sudden pause, then a jerk of the head on both men. Their eyes rolled back into their head, and the lights flickered off and on inside the room. Even the music seemed to drown out with slang and different voices, making the bartender come out of the back and see what was going on with the jukebox. But there was nothing to find, so she went back to what she was doing in the kitchen.

Richard looked at Daiye with red eyes and tears in them. He was in mourning for Daiye, seeing him for the first time.

"I'm sorry . . . so sorry . . . you're a strong man. You've been through so much. I just want to give you a hug and make it all go away."

Daiye looked at the crying man with such concern, and he touched Richard's hand one more time, and took the tears right out of his eyes. They were now in the eyes of the stranger.

"My friend, it was horrible what happened to your wife, and it was never your fault. You shouldn't be here, but I know now that you can't help yourself. So there is only one thing to do to help the healing process." Said Daiye. As he finished wiping his tears away. He chugged all the alcohol on the table, including Richards, like a champ. He wiped his lips with his sleeve.

The strange man continued his say, while Richard looked in marvel without tears. This man was either a very serious magician, or he had unlocked the powers of God. He was able to take the feeling from him, and now he had ownership one hundred percent. "This will be the last drink you will ever have. Because you have a family to raise, only since you decided to drink tonight and not see your kids. I will give it to you in full, so that way you can learn, so you can *see* my friend."

He touched Richard again, giving all the alcohol consumption to the fragile father. Daiye stood up and dropped a hundred dollar bill on the table, motioning to the bartender, and pointing in a circle shape that made it obvious that it was all taken care of.

"It won't be so bad." Daiye came and patted Richard on his shoulder. Almost knocking the man on the floor. He was drunk as a skunk. "Before I go, I just want to let you know. You better be careful getting home tonight, don't drink and drive, and steer clear of the Wheelbarrow Man."

Richard just nodded, and was swaying back and forth, a smile was stained on his face, and watched the man that was now super blurry, walk out of the bar.

It was dark, and the hour hand was in front of the nine now. Which meant that if Rake hadn't showed up at her house, something must have happened. Perhaps he might be packing clothes; that could take sometime. Or maybe, October and Rake might have worked things out, and she was being ignored.

Ruth paced back and forth in front of the bathroom mirror. Checking herself, and making sure her makeup looked fresh. They could go on a walk, or maybe go down Swers bar and break the news to her dad right away. These thoughts were a little crazy for sure, but they were true, Rake was experienced in life, and he would teach her how to love in the right way.

Waiting sucked, especially when it was for something that you desperately needed.

So she got on top of the toilet and peered off into the direction of the old farmer's house. Come to find out, that there was a red light shining over there. It was like a scarlet eye in the night.

She ran out of the bathroom and into the kitchen, grabbing her purse and her keys. "I think I might have forgotten that I was supposed to meet him at his house."

Only now she was met with silence. Over across the living room, Ruth found all three girls stopped in the hallway, with one ear up in the air. They were trying to listen to something, but couldn't quite locate where it was coming from. Rachael put a finger to her lips and hushed her. The sound had grown features in Rachael's mind, sounding like it was long, and must have huge hands or feet, because when it moved at all, it made a dragging sound.

"I gotta go girls, I will be back soon. Please don't tear up the house."

"Will you please shut the fuck up already? I can't hear anything with all your penis breath coming out of your mouth." Snapped Rachael, it was meant to wound and get a rise out of the older sister.

It didn't work and Ruth instantly brushed it off. "It sounded like its coming from the attic. You're in charge, and if you need anything, don't hesitate to call 911." With that, Ruth was gone.

Rachael knew that her sister must be as dumb as a bag of hammers, because there was no attic.

* * * * *

CHAPTER

7

Ruth's drive was long. The darkness had fallen over Plymouth like a giant black tarp. The lights on the truck beamed on the road, cutting the blackness and making the green leaves from the corn stocks gleam.

The thickness of the corn was so obvious, that when Ruth pulled to the side of the road in front of Rake's house looked secluded and haunted. Of course she was going to go in and get her man, but why did the house have to look so creepy? As if something was sucking the life out of the place, because there was no color, the roof was caving in, and there was a smell of bile and a hint of sweet syrup.

What the fuck? Was all Ruth could think. Never had she been over here, but she always wanted to and now that she was here, Ruth wanted to leave. Not without Rake; she decided.

Sneaking up to the house and trying not to make too much noise was easy, but when she put the first leg up on the porch there was a giant creak. Being silent was the hard part, the steps creaked regardless of how slow she went up them.

She made it undetected. That was when she saw the light again, it blasted through a crack. It caused Ruth to jump, but not cry out; thank goodness. If she was going to catch Rake and October, she needed to be ready and unexpected. Ruth hoped she wouldn't find them making love, or sleeping in the same bed together.

Peeking through the crack, Ruth could see the living room, hallway, and a kitchen table. Red light lit up the rooms. There on the table, hands clawed themselves out of a book. They seemed to be the cause of all the red dancing around the room. It was like animated blood, sliding off the wallpaper.

It was a queer sight if Ruth ever saw one. Frozen in fear? Or was she curious? Then there was a noise coming from the back of the house. Someone was coming, something that walked off balanced and the joints cracked when it moved.

The trees were like spider webs on the blackness. Leaves were in heaps on the ground with dead things in them. October had been here before, yes, been in her own personal hell with the lumberjack.

"Thinking of me?" *A voice said. Familiar, but it still clutched at her with sever coldness.* "I'm here, just wanting to know what you think of my new look."

There in a great distance ahead, was something walking into view with a 'clop' 'clop' 'clop' sound. Hooves that had red hair grown over them, and horns protruding outward, with white eyes. 'Clop' 'clop' it closed the gap between servant and Boss.

"This is what humans think I look like, which is quite odd, because this isn't scary. What is scary, is the man that losses his soul because of too much pornography. He is doomed to pay the moment his heart commits adultery in his heart. Scary is the feeling that everything is going to be okay, when its not, and you lie to calm the heart. The devil has many forms."

There was a zipper where October's mouth should have been, burning into her flesh as it appeared, and she was her sixty year old self again.

"Thank you for your donation by the way, I knew you had it in you. All humans have evil in them. Look, I can show you." *Like a magician, the horned boss balanced a spinning crystal ball on his middle finger, like a professional athlete would do with a basketball.* "You see there, that is the Figgs woman trying to kill her daughters. She loves them with all her heart, but depression put her over the edge. She found my book, and I showed her the way."

Elizabeth Figgs stood in the kitchen with four glasses of orange juice. All four daughters were in the living room watching the game channel, with the volume way up. There was rustle a in a drawer, which was Elizabeth taking out a medicine bottle, where she opened and crushed the pills on the counter.

What would the death of your child accomplish? What sort of leverage would she gain with them gone? But the answers was plain, because she too had found the book named: The Boss.

Mixing the contents into the juice, Elizabeth was struck with the decision to call them in to get, or bring it to them.

"Hey babe, I have something for you in the bedroom." *it was Richard, her husband.*

Richard hoped, it was enough to get her attention off the orange juice. So when Elizabeth went for the bait, Richard had poured all the drinks out, and filled up four new glasses, while his wife's back was turned.

"My book only brings out what was already there, October. With you, there was a bad. You let it take the man that you ever loved, but he was a cheater, and cheaters always get what is coming to them."

There was a sound of something coming. It was that thing again, the undesirable thing that pushed the wheelbarrow with a screeching wheel. Towering over all, even over the horned monster it served. The sphere went dark, but it still spun atop of the red finger.

The wheelbarrow man carried one skull in it's contraption, trying to get approval for the catch of the day. Balls of light would've been the ideal way to represent somebody's soul, but this was a world that didn't belong to humans, skulls symbolized the person's soul and the Devil was after them. There were no words exchanged. Perhaps the Devil was unhappy with only getting one this time. Billionaires make billions, not millions.

He waved the thing away, motioning to do better next time. There was no time to waste on just one, he needed a legion of them. It made sounds when it moved, earth shattering sounds, like the T-Rex in Jurassic Park. Then the footsteps seemed to mute, then like a spirit, it went back to the world October came from.

"When you sleep girl, you get to see me, see me in all that I do. You must wake up and give me that soul in your stomach. Into the book it must go, with all the other souls, so when its time for me to go home, I can give this to my father in full." *The devil licked the zipper, on her face and gave October an awkward hug.* "No more than two hours left, and it will be time for me to go home, so you better hurry. Eat those children, slay those cheaters, and watch out for *some of my brothers.* They like to slow things down for me."

The Boss unzipped October's face, and she was gone from that place.

Richard got up from his seat, dizzy and drunk, he made his way to the bathroom and vomited in one of the toilets. The good thing about this place, is the stalls were always clean and up to date. He made a big mess in the toilet, but it could easily be cleaned up, and that made all the difference.

He flushed the toilet, and went to the sink where he washed his face with cold water. Doing this; made him a bit more sober. When you puke, you always seemed to feel better and cut half your intoxication in half. With water was like a small slap to the face, energizing and just what the doctor ordered.

It helped out a lot. There was no way he drank that much at all, just no way, but here he was like some baby that spit up. It was that man, that . . . Daiye, he told him he would hit him with a ton of bricks. Except when he touched him, all the alcohol when into him. The emotions of the man became his emotions. Richard saw why the stranger hadn't aged at all.

What the fuck was he? An angel? Daiye showed him his girls at home, sitting around the table eating without him, seeing two empty chairs. One of which was his, that he should be sitting in it right now instead of holding hands with strangers. All with the gift of Daiye.

Just then, the room seemed to be darker than usual. Only a small light that shown on him from the ceiling reflected off the mirror he was looking into, and the light from underneath the door of the bathroom seemed to be gone as well.

Richard sobered up almost instantly, because that was when he heard the faint sound of screeching and heavy footsteps, that seemed to be gaining. Without a doubt in his mind, the old drunk was hearing the sounds, louder and louder, almost making his stomach sick again.

His hands were over his ears now, as he turned to face the stalls. Then it stopped, it was just peachy now, just a clean, dark bathroom.

"Daddy!"

The word made Richard jump, because the author of that voice wasn't human. Sending him fleeing for the door, and come to find out that it was locked and was soundless as he beat on it.

"Daddy!" It said again, the voice was robotic and feminine, and somewhat familiar.

It came from a robotic doll, one where the

legs moved in front of each with each turn of the obscure gears inside its body. White hands made of glass, with red finger nails, were out stretched towards the scared man. It came at a slow pace, but was closing the gap nonetheless, letting out the word "daddy" every six steps.

It was the voice of Rachael, sending a fluster of bugs in Richard's stomach and up his spine, that he might end up shitting his pants. *How do you shit your pants in a bathroom?* That would be a question on anyone's mind if he were to tell them.

The door was locked and wouldn't even give a centimeter, because Richard pulled on it with all his strength – drunken strength – and still he could not persuade the door to open. He screamed and kicked , and pounded, and shoved, and still it didn't move.

A string was attached to the back of the doll, that lead into one of the back stalls. The fisherman was hiding inside. Not just any fisherman, but the wheelbarrow man. He had come for him, and he used head games, to make off with his soul.

A screeching sound went along with the dolls spurts and footsteps.

"Please! I'll do anything! Anything!" Screamed Richard. Who might he be talking about? The answer was so easy when you're scared, because it was God. Everyone calls out for God when they know that their lives are going to be in danger.

Just then, the door swung open. Causing Richard to fall flat on his ass, hitting his head on the floor with a loud 'thud'! But the booze made it where his head didn't hurt so much.

A man was caught off guard to find Richard falling out of the bathroom. "Dude, what the hell are you doing? I gotta take a fucking shit, get outta here you drunk ass."

Which was funny, because he reeked of hard liquor as he stepped over Richard and entered the not so dark or scary room. It took a few moments to see that the room was just the way it looked when he first walked into it.

"What the fuck is you problem? All the damn doors are locked." The stranger made his way down the row of stalls, checking each door as he went, and not having any luck. "Nobody is in these, are you some sort of sick fuck playing games on the poor people that need to drop the kids off at the pool!"

The last one was the one that was open.

The stall of the Wheelbarrow man.

Before the man could spout off more obscenities towards Richard, he was yanked into the stall by a giant claw. Catching a glimpse of the creature in the mirror, and it was indescribable but it had a red eye, the color of blood.

Sounds of screaming and the sounds of Richard's feet hitting the floor as he ran, echoed through the bar. He needed to be home, like right fucking now. The taxi driver knew it too, because Richard was saying "I wanna go home – I'll never drink again," over and over again.

* * * * *

CHAPTER

8

Henry sat at a table that was basically the whole room. At one point, John's father and grandfather held meetings at his own home to save on costs. It did well, bringing in passive income by the truck loads. So much you never have to work again.

The butler let that sink in – *never have to work again* – that was the cold hard truth. Now it was all the little girl's money, which he knew would surely be his if he couldn't locate her. Even though he fought with his master about their relationship, Henry knew it might be too late for Sophia. It shook him up inside his core.

Stacks of books surrounded him, along with a laptop that had a website on demons. Where to find them, how to summon them, where they came from. It was all here, but what the net didn't have, books helped the thinking train stay on track. John's will was also present, it lay atop of the Dr. Sleep title. If it hadn't been for that book, John and Horac would still be alive.

The first thing to do was research. Research on his master, research on the will, and research on how to find October Blu. Not only that, the reader might change appearances again, making this search failure.

What was paranormal communication anyways? What were the ways to communicate with the dead, besides with a OUIJA board? A greater question was, why was John Silence communicating with the paranormal?

An employer never has to tell why he is doing anything in the workplace, but why all the secrecy? Henry would find out soon, he was making progress, even though he had his doubts. It wasn't even dark yet, and he had started his research once that strange man; JH left.

Henry found out that John liked to write his name in a book after he had read it. Sometimes before, but that was on rare occasions, to show that he had indeed read a book cover to cover. A reader's habit. Only if John knew he would finish it, would he ever write his name in the book first. It would get rid of what Henry liked to call: *buyer's remorse*.

Henry's opinion was, there was not such things as ghosts or monsters, only demons that humans mistaken for those things. There were no ghosts, no spirits, no Ghostbusters. Priests could be considered the only one that could come anywhere near being considered a Ghost buster. No exorcism ever took place in history or at least in Henry's life, but he knew demons played a part in this world.

The butler decided that he might have to take all the information that he learned about demons, God, and the Devil himself . . . and use it. Salt was one effective way to repel demons, he learned that first hand from John, that it was an act of God. The thought of John was overwhelming heartache. After all the findings and writings about the demonic subject, Henry still couldn't find the time to bury the two bodies downstairs. That was gonna have to wait.

There *was* such a thing called a Salt-gun Something that – of course – shot salt out the end of it, like a sawed off shotgun would do. The gun was used for huge swarms of horse flies, to quickly stun them, so they could then get a killing smack. He would use those when he went out to search for the reader.

From the internet, Henry found a list of demons names that existed in the world at one point. Some had pictures and statues of them, ones the Egyptians thought might of looked like. Indians, Mexicans, and even Americans had their take on the way a demon was formed and named.

One demon was named Aopohis, a serpent demon that stalked at night, one that didn't sound so bad at all . . . during the day at least. There was Murmur who was said to be a great Duke of Hell, that rode upon a beast. It taught philosophy and can ask the dead any question, and the dead would answer. Dead men tell no tales, only his demon would make them talk beyond the grave.

Hecate was said to be a queen of witches. John called October a reader because she was, but also called her a witch when he had struck her across the face. How would a demon come into the world? The answer was obvious, because the Bible had stated that they were thrown from Heaven after a great war or argument. To the Earth was Hell's summer home.

John had once said that when a deal was made with the Devil, things came through the thin cracks of reality. So now, it would mean that October made some sort of deal with the Devil. More research would show that someone did make a deal, so they could live young and long, and magic power would be given to them. The soul of the person, and the souls of children, would be given in return.

Nuns were servants of God, wedding their Father in Heaven, and devoting their lives to him. Witches were the Nuns for Satan, and they too served and were married, and gave the souls by consuming it. The popular origins of a witch, was that they ate children to grow young, but grow old when they used magic, making them a perfect child killer. Not only that, but they seem to unwillingly change shapes and at times could raise the dead on certain occasions, but only for a short while.

"Jesus", was all Henry could say as he read the horrific information and probable facts of

– perhaps – a fictional being. *What does the Devil do with the souls when he gets them?* Henry thought to himself, it was a good question. He thought perhaps it might be the ultimate bash against God, but what if he were to use them for something else? Maybe some sort of currency, which was an off the wall accusation. Speculation was another word for gambling, and the butler never gambled money away.

He'll never doubt anything again in his life, because he saw Horac being possessed by the demon that the reader brought with her. What sort of name did *that* demon have?

It was decided to go onto social media and try to find out if he could locate this October Blu. Something that he never did, but these sort of sites always had a way to sign up, and get in. Money was never an issue, because Henry had all forms of it now. Checking, savings, portfolio income, passive, investments, and even had the gold and silver to back it up. It was his, Henry felt like Bruce Wayne for a moment, doing the detective work and being rich doing it.

After sometime, there were some failed searches on the name: October Blu. Even on the main search engines, just some colors and the tenth month of the year. But what he did find, was a Rake Blu. Perhaps one that could be related to the reader that has stirred up so much trouble.

There were other results, but there was the location that struck up some interest, almost like a light bulb over the head moment. Yes, there was the corn fields and the canals that ran through all the corrugates, and a picture of a man that looked taller and built like a fridge. A red beard covered his face, giving him a mountain man look, one that occasionally took a shower here and there.

The address and where to find the house was all there; in the profile. Henry wrote it down on a notepad, and knew to check there first. It was his only lead in all this mystery, and he was sort of left with no choice, but to go there. So he gathered all that he could that might help track down this Rake Blu.

A black bag, with two salt shooters inside. One real loaded gun along with a box of ammo, with more where that came from. A few books on demons and witches, and one book in particular just in case it came down to it . . . the Bible.

Ruth saw a teenage girl walking down the dark hall. "Crack and creak" was the sound her joints made, perhaps it was the weight of her stomach that was protruding out. She just couldn't take her eyes off the thing that walked lame. Like a horse that had a sprang in it's leg, or a person with the big toe missing.

Almost . . . but not quite . . . did Ruth cry out. Keeping herself calm, she watched as the girl's body opened up like an egg. Her legs were spread and her arms were out to East and the West, as the claws made of light reached inside. What was subtracted from the body was a skeleton – a very large one – with red hair still attached to the head. Some hair fell to the ground as it disappeared in the book.

Ruth turned away from the hole, out anger and quiet emotion. That was Rake, the man that she loved. The man that didn't show up at her house; like he was supposed to.

Well wasn't this that evidence?

What is going on? Was all Ruth could think. She should be checking herself into a nut house – like now. From what she just witnessed inside the colorless house. But wait .

. . a thought hit her. Like lightning it struck her brain.

Rake had told her that he had a gun inside his closet just in case he decided to commit suicide, or to use it on coyotes if there were any. The girl that loved the farmer with all her heart, was going to get so called weapon, and end the wobbly bitch.

They say when you lose the one thing that matters most, you become the walking dead. People all around this Earth are walking dead, and they become numb to the things that should make them squirm. They long for something that will never be there, and wait for a call that will never be received. Now Ruth was one of them.

Making her way down the steps of the porch, and creeping around the back of the house. Tears had escaped her eyes, making her a blubbery mess, with her lower lip up, resembling a duck's beak. She was a beautiful crier. Even her sisters told her that, because when it came to beautiful girls, the ugliness that they lacked, came out with the waterworks. There were only two windows in the back of the house, the bathroom window, which was way out of reach. The other one must be the main bedroom, and it was so low to the ground. It would be pie to sneak through that window.

The moon made it so easy to see, even the cornfield looked like it went on for miles. The blinds in the window were up, but the curtains were pulled over the window. All Ruth had to do was open the window and quietly get inside the room. Assuming it was unlocked

A short amount of time was all she had. Enough to get in, find the gun, and unload on the damn thing. The choice was to go from the inside and do it in the kitchen. Or, take the gun out the window and knock on the door, then do it. Ruth thought the latter was the safest and better decision.

All bedrooms were the same, no matter where you lived. They had a closet, a bed, and a dresser. The gun would be in the closet, either on the top shelf, or down deep in the back; somewhere. Not even the bright moon's eye could shine inside this dark house, and turning on the light would blow Ruth's cover. Perhaps she got caught? An icy chill went down her body.

Up the window went, without even the slightest resistance. Then the right leg was up and inside the house. Being tall was a huge plus when it came to top shelves, but this was like getting up on a horse without a saddle, her over sized breasts were probably bruised as they hit the window seal. Even with a bra and a sports bra over that one, it was a bit of a chore.

Now inside, Ruth looked and waited for her eyes to adjust. The red light was still going on in the other room, so she was still good on time, but it did nothing to help Ruth see better, not even a smidgen. Nevertheless, she saw where the closet was, only it resembled a black hole. A black hole inside of a black hole, it was suffocating as she moved towards it, and felt around inside.

Clothes were making it difficult to feel around in the back, so she pushed the hangers slowly to the left and the right. Sweat went down her face like wax on a candle, as she pushed and dug through the clutter. Then there was a small voice, way deep in the back of her mind, that seemed to be getting louder and louder. Was the voice singing?

"She's mine, she's mine, I'll keep her all the time . . ."

It was an eerie tune, one that was catchy and new. With every word sung, sharp pains exploded in her head, making Ruth hold one hand to her temple. She continued to search.

"One time I spent the night, to keep her, that is my right . . ."

"Two dogs tried to run, when I pumped her in the bum . . ."

There! She had it. It felt like a gun, leaning to the far left of the closet. Her hand wrapped around the barrel, and she pulled. The song was making it hard, with every new verse, the gun seemed to be stuck. It took strong will and some balls from Ruth to use both hands, and pull the piece of metal and wood free.

It took her two tries, then it came out like the cork out of a wine bottle, shooting her backwards onto her back. Her landing caused a huge noise, one of which caught the attention of the thing in the living room, the girl with the white book.

However, that wasn't important right now. Because, even though Ruth had the gun over her, there was also something else attached to it. The darkness still made it hard to see, but there was indeed something hairy that was straddling her body. Ruth could feel it's weight of it with her breasts.

A head that was equipped with sharp teeth, a forked tongue, and a snout that made it resemble a lion. A beast from Hell, with white eyes that glowed in the darkness, which helped the facial features come out of hiding. Horns grew out of the forehead like a triceratops. Still the thing carried on its song, almost through a telepathic torture, and the pain was major and worse, with the beast at point blank range.

Then it seized it's melody and jumped off her like a scared kitten, a perfect description of that because it was a cat. It dived under the covers, and watched as the girl with the huge tits lay there in a heart pounding reality check.

Ruth stood up as fast as she could – bad idea – because her stomach ached, it was the fear that was making Ruth sick. She could hear the cracking of bones coming her way. The murderer of her lover Rake.

This situation was a huge fucking mess. There was no time to think, or try to make sense of the consequences of what might happen if she too got caught by October.

Rifle in hand, Ruth felt around for the safety to see if it was on or not, hoping that when she pulled that trigger, something would come out of the end of it. Ruth had seen a lot of movies to know how a gun worked. She had the gun aimed towards the sound, which had stopped now, because the monster was visible in the doorway.

It wasn't a girl anymore. A demon instead, that had hair grown in all directions. The light from the moon showed the jaws of white and yellow. It was a sight, that if seen completely with the lights on, would make Ruth shit the bed.

The gun went off.

She wondered if there would be anything in the damn thing, and thank God there was. The rifle's recoil had taken her off her feet, and knocked her back out the window. The air escaped her lungs, as she married the ground, the passed out.

Just like before, the book had taken the soul form October's body. Opening her up, and it reaching inside, to pluck out the man that she once called husband. Rake was a lot larger than the young girl was, but the book wanted children overall. A soul was a soul. A donation all the same. It took few hard pulls, but finally Rake's skeleton came out and went.

A feeling of pleasure came and went as it was subtracted from her body. The October in the dream was no longer old and exhausted, but the October ate the innocent again. Being as young and as short as she was now, Rake looked like he could take her. Not anymore, the hunger had taken her instead, and Rake had been a victim of that hunger. Sex was used as a weapon, than an act of pleasure, because October got pleasure from the extraction of the corpse. A siren, with a deadly song. All men and children will hear that song, and crash upon the rocks.

October's over sized stomach was gone again, but the stress from it, still made her joints crack when she moved. Even though the red apples would put her back together, it still hurt like a bitch.

The name of Rake Blu was written underneath Sophia Silence, the recently deceased. It was a fascinating sight to see, October caught herself off guard; in reading other names in the book, by a sudden thump in the far bedroom. It caused the red light to disappear and the book dropped to the floor. Someone was in her room.

The transformation began with a sudden change in temperature, the floor seemed to push up on her feet, and time slowed down. All the demonic powers October had, was showing itself at the time when it was needed most. *Hail Satan!* Was all she could think, as she began to change.

Like a werewolf, October changed in the full moon. Her transformation was swift and painless, hairy and claws that were razor sharp, and horns that made a popping sound, as they surfaced and punctured the flesh.

She was a different sort of monster when Rake had made love to, her form was horrific as a Jerusalem Cricket out on a wet sidewalk. She was sly, but her knees still creaked. It didn't matter though, still October went through the hall with little to no trouble.

Claws and her head was in the bedroom first, then she saw the scared young slut, the one that fucked her husband. Through the window she must have come, because when gun went off, she saw the big tit girl fly through the air.

Instead of going black, or passing out, or dieing. October's whole upper half went in all directions. A scream had escaped her, before her head had landed sideways on top of the dresser, she could still see despite it being detached. October could see that the room was moving, which was the little red apples running on the floor and walls, screaming and crying. They were trying to put themselves back together.

Then she saw something else. A body scurried out of the sheets of the bed, and jumped out the window.

* * * * *

CHAPTER

9

The window was rolled down just enough to let some cold air in. The moon was full in the sky, it looked like an eye that rolled up into a black socket. The black mustang drank up the night sky and the moon, as it pulled out of the driveway of the mansion.

Dr. Sleep sat on the passenger seat, with Henry's bad down on the floor. A hand was placed on top of the bestseller as the car straightened out on the road. There was a full tank of gas in the chamber, because nobody ever left the house. So this was bravery at its best for the retired surgeon.

The Blu farm was in the GPS, and the car was moving in that direction. Henry would arrive there in about fifteen minutes, and he would . . . what? Hand over the book and say, "this is the answer to all your problems". It was a plan, one that could go fifty-fifty, good or bad. Why was he going through with this? Why was he going through all the trouble to help out a reader? John was dead. Maybe it was for self worth. That would explain a lot.

A trained dog never asked why he had to do what he was told, they just did. Even with the car's lights on, the night was thick as a roll of quarters. He was kicking himself in the ass now for not going out to just blow some money. It would've opened up the world a little bit more.

How could he have crippled himself so much from something that was so natural? The windows should have been paintings on the walls, because he was never going to go outside. What the fuck was he thinking? New personal goal, go outside!

While thinking this, Henry drove right by a yellow taxi, that had honked at the black mustang for having blinded the driver. The slight distraction almost made him pass the Blu house, because it had been time since someone had honked at him out of anger. When the yellow taxi turned down it's street and was out of sight, there was a small moment where Henry was listening to the sound of the engine. It wasn't constant banging noise, but it was smooth, and it was nice.

That was when his lights reflected off the eyes of a figure. It was hairy and it walked on its hind legs in the middle of the road. A huge red mane, like a lion's mane, making it visible enough to stab terror into Henry's heart. Making him swerve the car out of the way, and right into a ditch.

Water from the pipes still flowed heavily down the corrugates, because a certain farmer wasn't there to close them.

The corn was like a hug sink hole. Sucking and bubbling around the front of the car, as the whole front of it was completely underground, then stopped.

"The destination is on your right."

Daiye walked through rows of tombstones

in the Victoria's Cemetery. Things have changed since he came back to this place. There was a lot more headstones added, which made him sad. Of course, these weren't his thoughts.

He had freewill just like the rest of mankind. So like them, he was stubborn, and didn't do his duty of protecting his area of the Earth. From Heaven he came, to help out Plymouth, Victoria, United Farms, and a part of Winesville. The town of Winesville was still being talked with the higher ups. It was hard to manage things, when you have stubborn beings.

Still, the stubborn Daiye decided to wise up and take of the duty he was created to do. Many others like him, even now, let their area go to waste. But enough was enough, and when his father decided to come home, he would be able to say that he took on his responsibility. It has been almost seven years since he started keeping the peace - five minutes if you count it in Heaven's time. Down here, Daiye thought he had done an alright job of leading the humans down the right path.

When he got deep into the R's, he started to find two headstones that were set right next to each other. One was a tall statue of a woman holding a baby in loving embrace. The other was a stone baby in a basket, awake and with arms outstretched towards the visitor that came to see it.

The wife and child of James River, name of the man Daiye walked the Earth with. The wife was Bea River, and the baby was Carol River. In life and in death, they were together. Flowers were already in the pots next to the stones, but there was enough room for more. Sunflowers were in Daiye's hand, he thought they would light away the dark path. He placed them in both pots. James would've wanted this, and Daiye always made sure that these two are never forgotten.

The day will come when they will be risen again, and Daiye made sure they were payed respectfully, in the time being. The thoughts and feelings from James crept strong into the mind of the angel, making him weep and hug the still baby.

"I'm so sorry. From the moment I set eyes on you, I knew you were the most beautiful thing I have ever seen." Daiye's tears fell upon the face of the stone daughter. He reached out to the woman, and wept even more. "I miss you so much, my Bea. I would give anything to see you one last time."

Then there gunfire off in the far distance, and the angel named Daiye was back in control. He had to tell himself again that these were not his thoughts, there was nothing he could do about it. Except go check on that disturbance in Plymouth. One of an angel's abilities are to hear all, and yes he did. When you hear a call, you answer.

There was a moment where Henry was out cold from the minor impact. It didn't take much to put an old man out, when you were beyond fifty. But only for a few minutes. The engine was still making its noise, but the evidence of where the car was positioned, there was no way it was going to get driven out.

A trickle of blood came down the side of his cheek. It was warm and weird as it flowed down to his neck. *My bag?* Was all Henry could thing when he came to. It was still there on the floor, but Dr. Sleep was nowhere to be found. He went to look into the back seat, but when he turned, there was a twinge of pain that shot up to the top of his head. A result of whiplash.

Henry gathered himself, trying not to move his neck too much. Grabbed the bag from the bottom of the floor, he noticed that the GPS was still working and a little white arrow was pointing to his destination. At least he was here.

He needed to get out of the wreckage and see if he was still functioning right before going on with his plan. Getting his bag was okay weight on the right arm, and it didn't really effect his heck much. Both legs were okay when he stepped out of the car. The mud did ruin his shoes, but that was one pair that can be replaced. He knew something like this would happen, and was prepared for it.

He didn't have the book though, it must have flew out the window on impact. His damn neck, it would be worse in the morning. What came out in front of him? It could have been a large dog or coyote. It definitely wasn't ordinary, but whatever it was, it was gone.

Dr. Sleep was also gone, which was Henry's way of maybe negotiating with the reader. It was an alright plan, but now he was down to no plan at all. The old butler had to wing it.

It took a minute to make out that he was actually looking at a house. There was no lights on, and if you squinted enough, you could almost make out the windows and porch. It blended in with the night. This was the correct farm, though it was a struggle to convince himself.

Wet sounds was the sound of Henry's feet as he walked down the road towards the house, with bag in hand. There was also another set of footsteps as Henry walked, and those other footsteps stopped when he stopped. He tested out the theory by doing a small skip, and sure enough there was a skipping sound.

For a few moments, Henry didn't move. What sort of thing was making that sound? His eyes must be playing tricks on him, because he didn't see anything, Henry know something was following him.

Nothing.

So he took another step and there was an echo of that step. For every squish of his muddy shoe, there was a crunch; followed by a dragging sound. What sort of gun did he need to use for this sound? The salt gun? Or the real gun? Perhaps maybe if the thing decided to jump him, it would get blasted either way.

Then there was a melody inside of his head now. It went on like it was some sort of made up kids song, singing about some girl was his. With every word that it sang, the more his head felt like it was being crushed. One part of the song, described that it was following a man with a bag. It went like "Henry held a bag of goodies, a head in his hand, and that there was a girl with huge boobies".

Before the thing could got to saying something like the girl with huge boobs ran off into the corn, with the twin dogs at her tail. Henry reached into his bag and pulled out the salt gun, and with one motion; shot it randomly in the direction he thought the singing might be coming from.

A dust of rock salt swished and swirled and hit the side of the house with a crackle. The pressure of the blast was just enough to make Henry grab the barrel in recoil, dropping the bag on the ground. He was afraid that he might drop the gun, but didn't.

It didn't work, like it worked when John had used a handful of salt on the demon in Horac. However, it did stop the musician in his head.

No need to reload the gun, because it was

meant for horseflies. So before the cloud of salt evaporated in the air, Henry shot another cloud of salt behind him. This one seemed to have gotten something, because there was a groan and a cry, that sounded like a mountain lion might have gotten it's paw stepped on.

Bingo.

The light of the moon mixed with the white of the salt cloud, started to show the outline of a figure that was transparent at first, but then it slowly had got it's features back. Hairy, bulky, tall, and ferocious. The thing quickly got out of the way before it could get swallowed up by the cloud, but was quickly able to scurry enough through it and knock the old butler out of his shoes.

Gravel plagued his back with sharp pains in his back and cut the back of his neck, damaging it more than it already was. No sound came out as Henry's mouth gaped open in agony, the hand he placed on it was as useless as a middle name.

What *was* useful, was not letting go of the gun as he went flying. Another shot went off, letting another huge cloud of salt in the air. It stung his eyes as it billowed around him, but it was a necessary evil, considering that the creature was standing over him now. Just enough so the salt wouldn't touch it.

Predator and prey both gave that look to each other, the one that would indicate that one of two things would happen. One being that the prey was cunning enough to outsmart the predator, or the predator wins. Henry thought that he would be able to lift his heavy arm and aim it at the catlike monster.

Then his legs were clutched by claws that dug deep into ankles of the old butler. This time a noise came from his open mouth, as he was dragged from underneath the cloud. Fully exposed now, it took all Henry's strength to throw his arms up in front of him like a shield. Much good that will do.

He waited for more pain, screaming all the while, and encouraging the death blow. But it didn't come. The monster stopped and looked to see who else had come to the feeding. Other footsteps were heard as Henry's body went into shock, giving him momentary numbness to pain and silence. A shred of energy motioned him to roll from underneath the demon, to see a man lit with moon, wearing a suit and tie.

A hand was stretched out towards the thing, making the monster hiss and claw out at him. It did nothing to weaken the man's confidence, as he reached out and grabbed the monster by the hand. That action was met with a claw to the face, which indeed split open the flesh like dry skin.

He welcomed it, and within a few seconds the creature was on it's knees, like it had lost a game of; Mercy. It let out a roar that sent terror into Henry's blood, then fell to the ground into a deep sleep. When it was for sure not going to get back up, the man in the tie let go of the claw, then walked over to the downed butler.

"You okay?" Asked the man with red face. His white shirt had soaked up most of the blood. "It'll be alright, there is no need to be afraid anymore."

Henry just stared in amazement at the young man in the bloody suit. He didn't know what to say or do, only hold himself in a way that he thought; would put is pain on the back burner. Henry could tell the other man was in pain and was hiding it extremely well.

"Please, I need your help my friend. The names Daiye by the by." Dropping down on his knees, almost falling. "Take my hands my good friend, it will pass, I just need one touch – I beg you."

It was like flinching almost, but Henry dropped the gun from his grasp and held it out to Daiye. Like a starving child, finally getting the food and drink that it so desired, clasped his hand over the butler's hand.

"This is going to hit you like a ton of bricks."

Then the two men tensed up, and threw back their heads, making a dangerous gurgle sound with their throat. As Daiye's touch did it's work.

* * * * *

CHAPTER

10

*"Tune in next time for the season finale, where the
story comes full circle. Will Alice make I out alive?
This is Red Hot Scream."*

R achael knew she wasn't supposed
to be watching a show that was a little
graphic – by graphic meant, tits and ass, blood
and gore, drama and horror. Only the story
was so good. She wished the twins would
sometimes do their own thing, because all
they did was follow her, and never saying a
word. Rachael thought the graphic scenes of
the show might get them to say something.

Nothing, just like before. Hopefully, in adulthood, the twins would find a happy medium and give talking a try.

"Why do they have to do this to us?" Said Rachael out loud. Scrolling through the guide, and finding nothing interesting, except maybe the food channel. "I mean how the fuck do they come up with this shit? I know Ella, I should not be cursing. Its just a word, its not like its towards you or anything."

She got up to get a glass of water. Whenever Rachael watched her shows back to back, she neglected to give her body its magic liquid. All three girls were in their pajamas, a tank top with pajamas pants, and all their hair in a ponytail. Very relax attire, so they could keep their mind off the moving sounds. *Something* was making them. Curiosity killed the cat..

Whatever *it* was, *it* was huge, and *it* was still making noises. Which had gotten the sisters spooked, but came to the conclusion that it want threatening. So far, it had only been the noises.

Ignoring it worked for a time. There was a point when the sounds were following them. If one of them had to use the restroom, the sound would grow faint to the girls waiting in the living room, but loud to the girl in the bathroom. It was just the same loud banging sound.

It took Rachael awhile to get enough courage to go investigate the distraction. She of course didn't need to ask the twins.

"Who wants to find out what the hell is making that noise?" Asked the older sister.

The twins answered by looking at each other in a worried state.

"Well don't all of you jump up at once. I would gladly go myself, but I thought I would ask."

Rachael was still met with silence. She knew they were scared, but more afraid t stay put. Rule number one when surviving a horror movie, never split up. Rule number two, don't check on strange noises. Since they were all going, the second rule wouldn't apply anymore. "Put your shoes on."

Just then . . . there was a knock at the door, stopping them in their tracks. A pathetic knock, but it was there. Rachael hesitated the most, she found herself, and turned the knob. Barbara and Ella were hugging each other, and were snuggled up against Rachael's back.

Hoping it would shield them from what was behind the door.

Turns out there was no one. Just a yellow taxi parked outside with it's lights on.

Cold was the world when it finally came back to her. There was the smell of Earth and blood; filling up her nose. There were sounds of chanting in the window she just came out of. It sounded ancient, and some words were mixed in with the sounds of a clucking and squawking. A possessed bird was what came to mind.

Ruth's sight was clear once again, and this time she could see that three was red things with legs crawling as fast as they could back into the window. It sent a bolt of electricity through Ruth's body, making her dodge away, quick like a bunny, from the red things. A whole ten feet away now, she rubbed her eyes like a child would do when woken up in the middle of the night. All to get a better look of what was going on.

Yes she had shot the fucker, by pure chance too. The little red apples must be her blood, and the chanting had stopped. October Blu must be some sort of witch woman, and she must have eaten Rake. It couldn't be true. It would explain that even after Ruth had blown a hole in the woman, she was still alive to speak chicken squawk. What the fuck was she going to do now?

Just then she heard another noise, like the scratching of metal and flesh, then a gallop on gravel. Ruth couldn't make out anything that the darkness was hiding, only it was coming towards her. Two dark figures in the pitch neared the poor girl on the ground.

Ruth forced her eyes to adjust to the darkness, the moon wasn't enough, but with a stroke of luck; a yellow car drove down the road next to the Blu farm, shining it's light in Ruth's direction for a moment. Then it was gone. The moment the lights were on the property, she could see two black labs snarling a few feet away from her.

"Shit, shit, shit!" Was all that came out, before she got up and bolted towards the cornfield. Her vehicle was an option, but you make stupid decisions when you're scared. Both dogs had their skin pulled from their body. The animals looked like they were wearing old clothes, the way the skin was baggy and holy, with a lot of white bone underneath. Their eyes were robotic, the way they just stared at her. It was enough to get her moving, enough to attempt to put some distance between the dead and the living.

She had seen some shit now, the one that took the cake. The sharp blades of the corn stocks, cut and slashed at her face and hands. There was pain at her ankles as she ran blindly in the direction she thought could provide a safe haven for her. Could that be more of the corn's swords? Or could that be the dogs nipping at her as they almost got a hold of her.

The gun was left on the ground, back at the house. What good would it do anyways? Cuts on her cheek were screaming in pain, as the cold air was seeping inside. Her heart was pounding, and the field went on and on. They were coming for her, and she couldn't do anything to stop it. On a lighter note, Ruth ran as fast as she could, without falling, and she didn't show any sign of slowing down.

Stamina *was* starting to recede though, like it always does. Which slowed her down to a jog, then a walk, and then a halt. Her hands were on her knees, and the wheezing was in her lungs. Thank goodness she didn't have any chronic asthma or anything like that, otherwise she would've died regardless if she had gotten away. Most people with that condition never seem to remember there damn inhaler when it mattered.

Just a few minutes was all she needed. Let her lungs take a small power nap, before going again. Ruth listened as hard as she could, to sense the presence of the zombie animals. Intelligence separated us from the animal kingdom, now that they were the undead, that fact can be disregarded. The dog's animal instinct, strength, and hunger, would be heightened; making her the special on the menu.

Help me please! Was all that Ruth could think. She hoped to God, someone would come to her rescue. Damn her tired legs, damn them to Hell for not going on like she wanted. No matter who afraid you were, you gotta stop and rest before doing such a demanding activity. Being in shape had nothing to do with it, it just came down to total imperfection.

They *were* coming, she heard them. But what direction were they coming from?

Without warning an animal shot out from the corn and knocked Ruth down on her ass. The moment she fell, she was back on her feet. The corn did make it difficult to move, but the fear was motivating, and it got her going again.

Running in another random direction, Ruth found herself almost to a clearing. The sudden adrenaline made her head feel like nails were being driven into her ears. She could smell it. Ruth could hear it. Was it there thought? It was there.

Water. It was gleaming in the night's light. Helping the feeling that there was hope to this nightmare. Ruth prayed so hard that she would get out of this. "Please God, I beg you. I beg you so much that I would do anything to get out of this."

All three girls stood together in the door frame, trying to make sense of why there was a cab parked on the property. Halfway on the cement, and the other half was on the lawn. No driver or passenger was in the vehicle.

Rachael hated being the oldest of the twins, because it was up to her to go and find out. Ella wouldn't, neither would Barbara, only the bravery in Rachael's heart, would go check to see the cab. She pushed her sister's arms away from her shoulders. *I am not a shield, but a sword. That is all I needed to be, to get ahead in life.* If some fucker wanted to leave their Twinkie shaped car out on the lawn, she was going to see who it was, and have something done about it.

There was no one to be found though, it was empty. Rachael threw a puzzle look at her sisters as if to ask for help with this mystery. The conclusion was that they too knew nothing. Rachael opened the door and turned off the engine. Thinking, Rachael pocketed the taxi keys. As much as she didn't want to, the older sister was gonna have to call the police, to get this thing off the property.

"Not a damn thing. Don't worry guys, I'll see if I can get a hold of Ruth." Rachael began to walk back towards the house, when she looked up to admire the huge moon; that lit up the night sky. It was amazing the way the house looked in the white light, almost making the house look like a sketch, made with pencil.

Staring upon it was making her slow, then stop. It *was* beautiful. Only now, she started to really look at the details in the shingles and the metal compass that was at the tippy top of the roof. Now she was seeing something else up there too. An outline of a person, two of them. One resembled a very large man, with long hair that was parted in the middle, Rachael knew this because with the moon behind the house, the man's head was heart shaped.

The other one was on all fours, with a head that had a long beak on the front of it. Heavy twisted hair, out in all directions, like a tumble weed that was mounted on the head of a giant tiger. Both of them just stood and watched with their white eyes, that seemed to float in midair, like the coyote after he fails to blow up the road runner and gets himself instead.

Quickly, Rachael stumbled into the house and locked the door. The sudden burst of tears from the older sister, made the twins jump in surprise.

What did she see out there? That the only thought the twins shared together, as they tried to comfort their sibling. *What had frightened the toughest sister out of the Figgs family? What did she see?*

Daiye finally let go of the surgeon, snapping him out of the same shared spasm that was done to Richard at Swers Bar. Only this time, the poor stranger in the tie, grabbed his right arm and held it close and hard. It looked like he was having a heart attack, the way he held his arm.

Henry snapped back to reality and saw he was still at the Blu farm, and that there was a man that had spoke the truth, about being it with a ton of bricks. What Henry saw, brought the old man to tears. What he seen and felt when the man had touched his hand – though it was very choppy – had also touched his soul. The pain in his neck and ankles were no more, even for a long afterwards, was the death of John Silence.

This man had taken it all away from him.

Based on the look on Daiye's face, that arm looked like it was eating him alive. The slashes on his face were healed and hadn't seemed to have any trace that they were there at all. Every injury done to Henry and the man that said his name was Daiye, was now living inside that right arm.

"Sorry about that my friend. To receive, you have to give, so I say sorry that I don't have a happy past." Said Daiye. He crawled towards the demon sprawled out cold on the ground. "Nasty thing I've ever seen. Would you believe me if I told you, he was my brother."

"What did you do to me? What is that thing?" asked Henry, wiping the tears away from his cheek.

"That was the part that you never get to see, as I get to. Give me a second, then we'll talk." Daiye reached over the monster's heart and placed his and on it. There was a moment that nothing happened at all, but soon the arms and feet of the monster, began to move and jerk. A roar of a lion came from the demons mouth as the pain emptied out of Daiye's right hand, and into the heart of the fallen angel. It took all but a few seconds to make the transfer, then the demon fell apart, into a pile of dust and ash, was lost among the gravel.

"This is a demon, Henry Fredrick, one that – despite him hunting the good – I love him with all my heart. I tried to save him." Said Daiye, he gave his right leg a smack and stood. Offering a hand to help Henry off the ground.

"Your an angel." Said Henry.

"That I am. I was sent here by The Three, to make sure you live a long and peaceful life. All of *this* – me and that monster – have been trying to do what is right, so our father will finally come home. Freewill has ruined us all, which caused my father to leave. I pray that one day, we'll all be together again."

"So you mean to tell me that God is gone. That that the lion looking thing is your brother, and you have daddy issues? I'm nuts. I'm going to the nut house, and I'm going to die in there."

"Everything must die my friend. It isn't Death you need to be afraid of, because that means you can come back. Its the Second Death that I'm concerned about. From dust you were made, to dust you will return. So now says The Three."

Henry gathered himself and his bag, this time he pocketed the real gun, just in case. "Now what? You just let me go, to live my life out to die of natural causes?"

Daiye didn't say anything for a long time. "Yes my good man. I think since we have this horrible thing call sin in the world, that going peacefully in your sleep is better than getting slaughtered by some fallen angel." The angel walked up to the Blu house and opened the door. "The reader isn't home. I don't know where she is, but I know that your master must have been reading fiction when he was speaking to ghosts."

The old butler sort of sank inside himself, hearing that was depressing. Now the butler really had no purpose to be here on the farm. Even so, he followed Daiye inside the dark house.

"This is so evil. There is something that is sucking the life out of the this place." Said Daiye.

It smelled of shit so bad in the house, that it was tickling the hairs inside the two gent's nostrils. There on the floor of the dining room, was a sliver of red light, sprawled on the floor.

"I see this has gotten away from its home." Said Daiye, as he picked up the white leather bound book.

"That was in a desk at the Broken Pane. That is why I'm here." Said Henry, he didn't know if he should feel relieved or be afraid. He must be both.

"Yes of course. I was the one that put it there in the first place. All snuggled up in a roll up desk. The other part of me wrote this book."

"You wrote it? How?" Said Henry, he was now confused as he'll ever be in his life. That is another story, for another time.

"If I wanted to be caught, I would have made it so. I wanted this book to be forgotten to the best of my abilities. It can't be burned, or torn, or lost. Only by way of being hidden among the other stories I thought it would make it disappear." Daiye opened the book and skimmed the contents. "I see that there is two new names, added to this book. Do you know who a Rake Blu is? Or a Sophia Silence?"

Henry's heart felt like it was breaking all over again.

"What if I do know those names?" Asked the old butler, tears had left his eyes as fast as they could.

"Then they're dead."

* * * * *

CHAPTER

11

When Ruth was at the edge of the water, a leaping sound from the corn made the poor girl turn around. Only to find a zombie canine knock her into the water canal. It was filled with mud, weeds, and fast moving ice water. The freeze made her gasp hard for air.

Ruth always wondered how deep these things were. Pretty deep, though she never thought she would end up in one. She went down, hit the bottom and was up again, and then the fast flow of the current was knocking her forward. Being constantly knocked off balance. Ruth quickly tried to float on her back, so she could at least try to see where see was going.

It was a success, but how was she going to get out? Up above the canal, were the two black labs running and barking, still trying to get at her. Ruth didn't know if she was safe or in danger floating toward an unknown destination.

Just then the two hounds leaped into the water behind her, doing the doggy paddle and gaining on her as she was floating at an alright speed. Ruth must out swim them, or they would get her. They were determined to get her, concentrating with such effort, to catch up.

The young girl did a flipping motion, so she could get on her stomach and kick with her feet. It was so difficult to do so, because it was so cold and weedy down below. Like hands they grabbed at her feet. A few times she got stuck and lost a shoe, to the fast moving canal. Bruno – although that was the dogs name, Ruth would never know that – was upon her and snapped, but missed. The second time the dog snapped, it got her shoulder, diving her down into the water.

The thought of drowning the black animal was a good idea, but Bruno didn't let go, and Ruth couldn't hold her breath. You couldn't kill what was already dead. Ruth was gasping and trying to scream at the same time, grabbing the side of the ditch and failing to hold on.

Faster and faster she was traveling towards a wall with a large pip in the middle. If she hit that pipe, she would drown if she got stuck. Despite the pain in her arm, even with the dogs head moving back and forth, trying to tear it off as she floated towards a pending death. Right before she hit the wall, Ruth turned and lifted her feet as high as she could get them. Squeezing the dog between her huge breasts, they both hit the wall. Giving her what she needed, which was for Bruno to let go.

When there was nothing else holding the dog to the young girl, Bruno was sucked downward, making him disappear into the pipe. It must have been big enough, so that the pipe didn't get clogged from the beefy body of the animal.

Exhausted, Ruth was holding on with great effort to the wall, trying not to get sucked in like the thing with four legs. It wasn't over just yet, because there behind her was another dog by the name of Einstein – Ruth couldn't have know this either.

The brother of the two labs, was coming fast on Ruth's back. There was a ten second window, where Ruth tried to attempt to climb up the wall of the canal, her foot almost getting sucked under. Luckily she was able to place one foot on top of the pip, but it fell, when another set of teeth bit into the same spot as Bruno did, making her go under.

Under the muddy water, the two fought each other. Einstein had a good hold on her, and she was running out of fight and air.

The pull of the pipe was strong and all her attention was on getting the beast of her back. Making her aware that she needed to make the decision to win, or to lose. The obvious choice was to live, but it was so hard. Ruth was exhausted.

The image of Rake came into her head. He was wearing a clean red button up shirt, and a golden belt buckle, and it went very well with his cowboy hat. The beard on his chin was red, thick, and long. God she longed to put her hands through it again. Perhaps it was the lack of oxygen to her brain that made her see the man she loved, and she was gonna see him soon if she didn't fight this fucking dog off of her.

That did it, Ruth took all the strength that she had left, and did a 180 with the black lab, so the pull of the pipe grabbed the tail of it first, releasing the bite on her shoulder. Her shoulder burned like Hell. She tried to get to the surface before she was sucked into the pip along with Bruno and Einstein. With much effort and almost drowning, Ruth made it.

Sophia was dead. The fortune was his. Now, he wished he had fought better to be a better father figure for her than John had been. His master gave up too easy, which was a horrible trait to have when you are raising children. Henry prayed for Sophia, except it would do no good. When you run away, there is no way someone so young could make it on their own, especially in a world with an economy like this.

"I know your pain Henry, it is so unfortunate that youth has to leave this world. Only she will be okay without pain. Death is only a long nap. She will be in your arms again." said Daiye, he had shut the book and ran his hands through the old butler's hair.

"I don't know what to make of all this, I'm lost, and everyone around me is dying." cried Henry.

"If I touch you again, the way I did to heal both of us, you would see that what I say is true."

"You showed me nothing but a sad part of a man that you once were. that isn't going to help bring the dead back to life."

Daiye thought a moment before answering, because he wanted to let the poor man know that him being there with him, was a good thing. "I am two people, yes, but I am an angel of the Three, they have sworn that all humans will be protected by an angel no matter what. Problem is, there is only one of me and a couple thousand of you.

I saw in your heart, that you came here to save that reader. I'm telling you that you cannot, unless we know where she is."

Henry stayed silent and listened to the angel go on.

"I'm not a very good angel to be honest. It has to do with freewill and the departure of my father.

I try to help to the best of my abilities, just

not too long ago, I had helped out a drunken man by taking the grief from his dead wife. I showed him, like I showed you, that as long as you have love, you can do anything."

Daiye looked at the book, then held it close to himself. "Its all my fault that this happened. If my book had never been found, it might not have ruined the lives of so many people."

Henry was taken aback. "You mean to tell me that you wrote that book?"

"Yes, but it wasn't me that made it so evil. It was my first novel as a writer, and somehow it had gotten swooped up by an evil demon that changed it to the book that you see now. I didn't even name it The Boss, I hadn't even given it a name, because all the good titles for love stories were all taken."

"This doesn't make any sense angel. Your either lying to me, or making up stories. I must be losing my mind if your two people." Said Henry, he was walking down the hallway, just so he could get some breathing room from the man in the suit.

"You're not losing your mind. Haven't you ever heard the phrase: *touched by an angel?* I'm actually touching your soul, but you will always see me for what I am."

"You really do look like a lion?"Asked Henry, he had seen Daiye's past.

"Not all of us look like lions, but yes, I and many demons and angels look like the animal called a lion. If I looked like my true form, I would frighten the people I wanted to help."

It was starting to make sense to Henry. That thing that caused him to wreck his car, was a fallen angel, now called a demon, and kept its true appearance was a lion. The *touch* part made Henry believe that the man named Daiye was truly telling the truth, that there was no way he was going to help that reader. No way he was going to help October Blu.

"You said something about, if we knew where the reader was?" Asked Henry, he grabbed the tie around Daiye's neck and pleaded.

"Let us walk down this hallway and see in the bedroom. Some witches leave traces and I think there might be some activities in there, I now this from personal experience. But that is a story for another time."

Daiye placed a hand on the back of the old butler's back. It was also hard to be afraid when you are being escorted by an angel. Of course, Henry was though. The angel switched on a light, and found that there was an opened window, a closet with all the contents spilled out all over the floor, and a bed with messed up sheets.

"Look there Henry, on the floor below the window, what do you see?" Daiye was pointing and had an eye closed.

Henry hesitated, but walked over to where Daiye had motioned towards, and after a few seconds saw a what appeared to be a tiny red apple. Like a red ant, but this was indeed a fruit that had arms and legs, it ran around in a circle like it was in a panic.

"What is it?" Henry found a glass from the dresser, and placed it over the red thing, trapping it and observing.

"Its blood, it got left behind from that reader you talk about. She is wounded. But as long as those things are eating something, they can live for a very long time. There hasn't been an evil like this in a very long time. Henry, we might have our work cut out for us."

"Work cut out for us? What's this *us* you keep talking about? Isn't you who have to fight your own kind? I can't do anything against them, I'm just some retired surgeon."

"You're a very wealthy surgeon to be correct, and I never said that this fight was only between angels and demons. Humans need to pick a side and fight alongside them, not human vs. lion, it is lions with humans that will bring the world to peace. We only have a short time before The Three make their decision to end the war."

It took a moment to think about sides, lions, and humankind. What would he have to do now that he knew all this new information?

Daiye walked over to the glass and lifted it off the tiny apple. He picked it up and smashed it between his thumb and pointer finger, making a popping sound as he did it. Doing this, must have reminded him of something if true importance, because the angel seemed to be frozen for a few seconds. He spun around and grabbed the arms of the old butler. "We need to find her family."

"Who's family?"

"Richard Figgs' family. We must go and see if he has gotten home safe. I heard a prayer just off in that direction." Daiye pointed through the wall of the house.

Confused, Henry's eyebrows showed that emotion. "How do you get that from squeezing apple?"

Daiye grabbed the jacket, that was Henry's, and dragged him in the direction of the exit.

Putting her foot back up on top of the pipe and resting for a bit, was an awesome feeling. Maybe she would get out of this alive, considering that the two dogs were now long gone, Rake's wife was blown in two, and her body was in shock. Making her shoulder numb, which was really good on her part. She needed to go to the hospital, but she also needed to just lay down in the dirt for awhile, to regain some strength. Ruth surprised herself when she was able to pull herself out of the canal. Water fled off of her clothes, releasing some of the weight, which saved her. Ruth had survived. Her injury though, kept her from forgetting to get help as soon as possible, but it would give her a few moments to stare up at the stars.

Orion's belt and the Little Dipper were always her favorite. Besides the Sun,

Betelgeuse was her favorite star. A song from The Wizard of Oz popped in her head, the one about the rainbow, a celebration song, that put a smile on her face for a little while.

Without warning and without sound, Ruth saw a figure out of the corner of her right eye moving through the corn. She should of stood up and started running, but instead she tilted her head to see if she could see it better. Sure enough, there it was. The old farmer's wife had taken on the form that turned the stomach of Ruth.

October stalked her prey.

* * * * *

* * * * *

End of part 2

* * * * *

Like what you read?

Check out The Broken Pane, the first book in the Not For Kids Series.

Support an author instantly by leaving a review on Amazon.com. Put the name Jorge Harrington in the search bar and click the title of your choosing, then leave an honest star review. This honestly is the best way to help local or popular authors, and I just want to say thank you for taking the time to read not only this book, but leaving a review for me. Keep on reading, thank you from the bottom of my heart.

You can contact me by email, Twitter, Facebook, or Instagram. All that information is

jorgeharrington032089@gmail.com

Jorge Joseph Harrington on Instagram

@geobonii on Twitter

Coming Soon

The Man That Couldn't Die

Not For Kids Series

Vol. 3.

www.ingramcontent.com/pod-product-compliance
Lightning Source LLC
Chambersburg PA
CBHW020137180626
46810CB00004B/1595